The Perdone Collision

by

John B. Wren

ISBN: 978-0-9889371-8-5

IN MEMORY OF MY FRIEND,

GAIL BOND LORD

*   *   *

Also by

John B. Wren

To Probe A Beating Heart

Killing His Fear

Darryl's Reunion

an Trodai

*   *   *

PREFACE

"Now, my own suspicion is that the universe is not only queerer than we suppose ... but queerer than we can suppose ..."

JBS Haldane

Questions are abundant when discussing the universe and answers are not all forthcoming. For thousands of years, we wondered about the sun and the moon, the stars and other celestial objects. As science grew and we developed the tools, the physics and the mathematics to better analyze that which we observed we have become more aware of that which we don't know. We now recognize our little planet is not the center of everything, we are a small rock orbiting a medium star along with several other planets and a plethora of asteroids and comets in a galaxy that is one of billions in the known universe.

The mysteries solved open doors to more of the same and now we wonder if our observable universe, supposedly generated by the Big Bang some thirteen billion years ago is the only one to ever have existed. Could there be other universes far beyond our ability to see? Are there an infinite number of such universes? We may never know.

The premise of this story is encountering an alien race from a close, dwarf galaxy on a collision course with the outer reaches of one of our galactic arms and learning of other alien races scattered throughout the observable universe and beyond. The ability to travel great distances at speeds in excess of light speed is attributed to the harnessing of a form of dark energy as are the weapons used by the aliens.

The internet was a source for much of the information read in writing this tale as well as the books I have collected. I thank all those who have gone before me in researching the cosmos as well as the counsel, criticism and praise of my editor, Tanya Besmehn. I further thank family and friends for their patience and advice, without them all, this book would not be.

John B. Wren

All that is written herein is not proven science, much is pure speculation pulled together to make a story. Is it all possible? Who is to say? It may be no more than my imagination spilling out onto the page.

Then again, the Talmonoria may be watching and listening …

~JBW

*   *   *

ONE

2245 AD

The universe is rife with galaxies of all sizes, many larger than the Milky Way, all moving in different directions as the universe continues to expand. Our solar system exists over 30,000 light-years from the massive black hole, Sagittarius A star, at the galactic center and approximately 20,000 light-years from its outer edge. Our closest large galactic neighbor is the Andromeda, about 2.5 million light-years away and on course to collide with our galaxy in about 4.5 billion years.

Galactic collisions occur with great frequency. However, the distances between the bodies within the colliding galaxies often allow one to pass through the other with naught but some gravitational effects on the various elements of each. Such has been the expected case with the passing of the Perdone, a dwarf galaxy, as it approaches our galactic arm of the Milky Way. The two rotating spiral galactic discs are at approximately 87 degrees to each other, and the centers are currently about 32,000 light-years apart.

We can see the outer reaches of The Perdone passing through our arm of the galaxy approximately twenty light-years away, and further observations lead to the conclusion that several planetary collisions are more than possible. We watch and observe smaller asteroids being affected, pulled by the nearby stars or black holes; some have been forced in the direction of our solar system over the last several thousand years, and many now cluttering the already over-populated layers above Earth. Some pass through, some enter the upper atmosphere of Earth where they burn up or fall all the way to the ground, and others settle into Earth's orbits. All of these are a problem, and the International Space Authority patrols the various layers in older shuttlecraft, collecting the smaller bits and redirecting the larger masses out of harm's way. Mars and Saturn have both been favored dumping grounds for thousands of tons of this "space rock." Man-made materials and rarer elements, when found, are collected for both Earth and space-based processing facilities.

The world has been at relative peace, discounting a few small squabbles for more than fifty years and the task of collecting the bits and pieces of invading material has fallen to military pilots who have few tactical targets to investigate or destroy. They maintain their piloting capabilities in part by flying shuttles between the planet surfaces and the several rotating space stations as they manage the influx of asteroids, and meteors, and collect space trash.

*   *   *

2245.08.13.11.06 (Zulu) Earth orbit, sector 23.14, J level Aboard shuttlecraft WSA-C-3459

Jason engaged the winch retractor, pulling the largest piece of this target, an old solar panel, in through the shuttle's open bay doors. He then touched his com-link, "Target inside the bay, Captain, you can close the doors." He maneuvered the large panel against the bulkhead and strapped it in as the doors slowly closed and a green light signaled the airlock hatch opening.

Darce tapped the intercom, "Sarge, are we secured?"

"Aye, Captain," returned Jason as he glided into the airlock, pulling the hatch closed behind him and pressurizing the small space. He checked a control panel and tapped his com-link, "Target secured, airlock closed and pressure stable." He removed his gloves and helmet and began removing his EMU.

"Got it," returned Darce, "come on up."

Jason opened the interior airlock hatch, pulled himself through, closed the hatch, stepped out of the remainder of his EMU and secured it against the bulkhead. He pulled himself through a hatch to the passageway to the flight deck, "What's next, Darce?"

"Call it in and see if they have another piece of crap for us to catch," said Darce.

Jason buckled in and tapped the com-link, "Station SW-23 Command, C-3459 secured. Do we have another target?"

"C-3459, make contact with SW-27 Command, they have something for you to look at."

There was a slight pause as Darce started punching the connection code for SW-27 when his com-link lit up, "This is SW-27, Captain. We have a big one for you to check out," replied Station Command. "Object DD-1826, a chunk of rock we think may have come out of the Perdone, approaching one level up and one sector over from your location."

"Copy that," returned Jason.

"Just how big is that thing?" quizzed Darce, "The data I've seen indicated it was relatively small and would pass through the M or N Level. Shouldn't be a problem. We have mostly nuts, bolts, a few rocks, and two old solar-power panels in our cargo bay, so there's plenty of room."

"What are you flyin', Captain?" asked Station Command.

"C-3459, it's an older shuttle with a 120 cubic-meter bay," returned Darce.

"This is way too big for your cargo bay gents, but we'd like a closer look," said Station Command, "1826 has been on course to pass us within the next several hours, but we noticed a slight variation in its heading and speed about an hour ago. Might have hit something after coming through Kuiper, could be breaking up. We just don't know. Like you to get as close as you can and verify some of these readings."

"Copy that," returned Darce. "Feed us the coordinates, and we'll give 'er a look."

"Coordinates entered," said Station Command, "let's do a chronometer check before we proceed."

"Copy that," returned Jason. "On your mark."

"Chronometer reading Zulu, 2245.08.13.11.48.00 in 4, 3, 2, 1, Mark," said Station Command.

"Confirmed," said Jason. "Now when we finish this one, it's three weeks back on the surface. Really lookin' forward to a little R&R."

"Yeah, sounds good to me too," returned Darce. "I gotta check in with a few old contacts, see if any of them remember me."

"What? We've only been gone six months," said Jason. "Any storm in port."

"You mean any port in a storm?"

"Ha, you find a port, I'll find a storm," said Jason with a wicked grin.

Station Command transmitted the coordinates. "Captain, this thing is moving at about 0.65 LS Negative 4, and if it's breaking up ... well, be very careful."

"Copy that, 0.65, eh? She's movin'," said Darce. "This old buggy might be able to hit .7 LS Negative 4, (46, 872 mph) but that's really pushin' it."

"Understood," returned Station Command.

"Station Command, coordinates received, I'm beginning to adjust," said Darce as he punched in the copy command and energized the thrusters. The shuttle nose lifted, and the craft came to the new bearing. As Darce brought it to the K Level, he tapped the com-link, "K Level, Sector 23.14, please advise target location."

The reply was immediate, "Object DD-1826 is about forty-two seconds out. Your location is confirmed, maintain current speed and change course on your heading, bearing 37, lift 4 degrees."

"Copy, Station Command," returned Darce ... "time check?"

"Thirty-five seconds."

"Copy," said Darce. "Any further description? Like is it flashing red or blue?"

"Negative, no energy readings, no detected life forms," replied Station Command, "just a big dirty rock like Oumuamua ... 23 seconds."

"Copy that. How are we lookin'?" returned Darce.

"Your speed is good, Captain. Come to bearing 317, lift negative 3 degrees, and standby to accelerate to match object," said Station Command.

Darce energized the starboard and topside thrusters bringing the shuttle to its new heading.

"Looking good," said Station Command, you're running parallel about 300 meters off your port side.

"Got it on my sensors, should be visible in a few—there she is," said Jason. "Just like you said, a big dirty rock. Oumuamua was back in '017. Is this a return trip?"

"This one ain't big enough," returned Station Command, "you notice anything else?"

Jason responded, "One large chunk of rock, no tumble, no rotation."

Darce added, "I'm beginning to increase speed."

"Careful Captain, can you run parallel?"

"It has just moved past us. I'm in catch-up mode," returned Darce. "It looks way too regular in shape to be a natural, dark-colored rock with a rough surface."

The shuttle lumbered ahead straining to reach speed as Jason scanned the object and listed the readings, "Dimensions: roughly 9.2 meters in length, 4.6 meters wide and 3.2 meters high, but not able to get a decent reading on its mass. It's bouncing between 4,000 and 5,000 tonnes."

Control Central, located on the planet's surface, joined the conversation, "Captain Gannon, Colonel Sarah Hansby here. Are you getting anything other than normal readings?"

Darce looked at Jason, "Nothing unusual Colonel, we'll stay with this thing 'til it's out of our neighborhood."

Jason chimed in, "I'll send some visuals in a few seconds. Maybe we could hit it with our Super-Secret Space Rock Destroyer."

Darce laughed, "Yeah, if only we had one. We might be able to cut it into smaller sections, if we had the time."

Colonel Hansby commented, "You don't have any weapons on that old cargo wagon, do you?"

"No ma'am," laughed Darce, "just thinking out loud."

Sarah Hansby chuckled, "A Super-Secret Space Rock Destroyer?"

"Sure, Colonel," said Jason, "an SSSRD."

She laughed, muttering, "Crazy Marine flyers," and followed with, "Jason, you give me a good design, and I'll build you one."

Jason linked his scanners to the stations main system and was looking out a port when he suddenly interrupted the Colonel, "Ma'am, target is slowing down. We're down to .62 and dropping."

Hansby barked into the com-link, "Station Command, is it maintaining direction?"

"Negative," replied the SW-27 Station Command. "It's dropping through the K Level, Captain Gannon do you have a speed?"

The object was slowing and losing altitude. Darce checked his control panel. "We're at .56 and dropping," he said, looking again at his control panel.

"Stay with it, Captain," said Hansby.

"Aye, ma'am," returned Darce as he guided the shuttle to a new heading, "passing through .50."

The shuttle's sensor readings began to fluctuate wildly. "Hey, are you guys getting this?" Jason shouted into the com-link. "The mass is increasing. That's not possible." He pinned the readings, then sent them to both Station Control and Control Central. "Course change! It's moving to a lower level."

"I see it, Sergeant. This doesn't look good," said Station Command. "Captain, have you opened a channel to the object?"

"Tried," returned Darce. "No luck. We have a hailing message on a loop. Nothing."

"Captain, we have you parallel to the object," said Station Command.

"Copy that," said Darce. He looked at Jason, "What are you seeing?"

"1826 flying alone … no debris, no friends."

Jason pointed at a display on the control panel.

Darce tapped the com-link again, "Hold on. The damn thing is up to something. Jason's reading another large mass change."

Station Command responded, "Please repeat, a large … what?"

"Sir," said Jason, "its mass just increased by a factor of 9.86."

The object suddenly dropped straight down toward the Earth's surface. "I'm losing it," said Jason. "It's through F Level and dropping."

"I can't keep up in this trash hauler," said Darce. "Target's going nose first in a controlled flight. This ain't no damn rock! Recommend a tactical bird."

"Already on the way," returned Station Command. "Maintain current altitude, bearing 176."

Three tach birds disengaged from Station SW-27 and SW-23's outer rings and spread out to intercept 1826's predicted path. Each tach bird was equipped with four conventional missiles and two additional missiles with tactical nuclear warheads.

"We'll use one of the missiles, if necessary," said Hansby, "but we're getting very close to the surface."

"Maybe too close," said Darce.

"We're watching the mass changes," said Hansby. "You're right Captain, we're too close to the surface for the nukes. Wait till it's over water then … maybe we open up on it."

Darce grumbled as he adjusted course, "A trash hauler. Dammit, we should be in a tach bird."

"I heard that," said Station Command. "Captain Gannon, your presence is required on board SW-27. Command wants both you and Sergeant O'Leary in the briefing room ASAP."

"Aye sir," Darce adjusted course toward the station and increased speed.

* * *

As the shuttle approached SW-27, the Station Command portal controller opened his com-link, "C-3459, we're ready in the middle ring, portal B-3."

Darce looked at Jason, "You ready?"

"As ever was," returned Jason.

Darce opened his com-link to the portal controller, "C-3459 approaching DP-B-3."

SW-27 is a rotating, three-ring space station with four docking portals on each ring. The portal controller responded, "Got you on scanner, Captain. Rotational speed 16, clamps out and ready. Rotate negative 90 degrees and come on in closer."

"Matching rotational speed at 16," said Darce, "aligned with portal and moving to first two clamps."

"Copy that," said the portal controller, "contact in ten seconds."

"Forward clamps in view and aligned," said Darce. "Contact ... bring me home portal."

The portal controller guided the fore clamps to the shuttle's connection collar and made contact. A heavy metallic sound reverberated throughout the hauler. The controller changed his view to the aft clamps. "Aft clamps aligned," he said, "contact in four."

The aft clamps made another loud sound, and Darce said, "Aft clamps contacted, I'm cutting power. You have control, portal."

"Copy that," said the Portal Controller, "standby for final connection."

The shuttle was pulled the last few meters to the belly of the station and locked in place with another meshing of metal parts. "C-3459, you are home and secured. Rotational gravity should be about .946. Release your cargo bay doors and come aboard."

Darce and Jason pulled themselves through the tube from the flight deck to the cargo bay, opened the airlock hatch, and reached for the ladders being passed down through the bay doors. As they climbed up to the station floor, Jason noticed several high-ranking officers and a slight mechanic hurrying across the open space.

"What's the rush?" asked Jason.

"Probably the big meeting in the briefing room," returned Darce.

The mechanic, turned and stared at the two newcomers, "Who's that?"

"The C-3459 crew," answered the Portal Controller, "Captain Gannon and Sergeant O'Leary. they're off SW-23."

"They're not in uniform," said Kearsay, "which one is Gannon?"

"The tall one," responded the Portal Controller.

Darce was a solid 6'-3" with light brown hair broad shoulders and dark blue eyes. Jason was an even 6'-0", built like a linebacker with black hair and brown eyes.

"Make sure they're both in the briefing room," said Kearsay.

As the group moved on, Darce and Jason approached the Portal Controller. "Welcome to SW-27, gents," said the portal controller. "You have anything for me to off-load?"

Jason pointed at the solar panels and shrugged, "No big rush. Where's the briefing room?"

"Follow the crowd," said the Portal Controller, nodding toward a group of white lab coats.

Five minutes later, Darce and Jason were in the briefing room with a dozen other pilot and navigator crews along with about 50 other officers and the people in white lab coats.

* * *

TWO

2245.08.13.11.52 (Zulu) Briefing Room B-04, Aboard SW-27

General Kearsay, a tall, thin, silver-haired man, entered the room with his aide, Major Tetra Harmon. She looked like an overworked mechanic, dressed in coveralls, covered in dirt and grease. She stood next to the General, wiping her hands on a towel. Kearsay picked up a pointer and energized the viewing screen as the crowd went silent. He addressed the audience, "This is a download from C-3459's scanners," he paused, spotted Darce in the crowd and continued, "as Captain Gannon approached to a range of approximately 100 meters, the object dropped to an altitude of 65 kilometers, well within the D Level, turned in parallel to the equator and made a complete revolution of the planet in less than 40 minutes, and it maintained a constant altitude." He looked at the audience, "Then it shot back up to the K Level, completed a half-loop around the Earth then headed back in the direction from whence we think it came."

Darce and Jason both nodded in agreement as Colonel Hansby tapped in, "We didn't get a heat signature or any energy readings. This thing showed as a cold lump of rock." She paused for a second and continued, "There's more. Instrumentation on the surface indicates that we've been scanned, most probably by the object."

"Scanned by a hunk of rock," puzzled two people in the audience simultaneously.

"Apparently much more than an asteroid," replied Kearsay.

"Yes," said Hansby. "Something of intelligent design and control."

The muttering in the room rose, and Kearsay tapped on the podium, "DD-1826's trajectory has it most probably originating from a system in the Perdone Galaxy. That's over twenty light-years away. We're focusing our sensors in that direction as we speak."

Three people in white lab coats entered the briefing room and took seats near the entrance. Kearsay saw them and nodded as they took their seats.

Eunice Carlon raised her hand, "Sir, we didn't see 1826 until it appeared coming out of the Kuiper belt. We didn't sense anything other than a big rock moving at 0.2LS-3 following a gravitational path that indicated a possible impact on Mercury in a few months. Then, as it approached the Martian orbit, it slowed to the LS-4 level and appeared to be on course to pass through the Earth's N Level. It was just earlier today that we noted another change in its projected flight path."

"We didn't get a power reading, or any different sensor readings from our scanners until it was as close as it was," said Kearsay. He looked to Major Harmon for an answer, "Why?"

Tetra replied, "We're checking back through the scanner files, nothing yet, sir." She stepped forward, "Assuming 1826 was moving at something less than LS-0, it would have left Perdone at least twenty years ago. Any speed greater than LS-0 would explain why we didn't see it until it passed through the Kuiper where it would have slowed to navigate through or around the belt."

Jason raised his hand and Tetra reacted, "Yes, Sergeant O'Leary?"

Jason spoke up, "As we approached it, there was a sudden shift in the gravitational readings. It was as if the damn thing increased in mass by a factor of ten then suddenly dropped toward the surface."

Harmon nodded to Kearsay, and he looked at the three scientists who had joined the briefing. All three nodded and he said, "We've confirmed those sensor readings here and on the surface."

The three nodded again, and one stood.

"Bennay Loehr, you'd like to add something here?" asked Kearsay.

"Yes, General," said the older man. "We have detected signals from many sources throughout our galaxy over the last three-hundred years. Some of these have originated near several stars in the Perdone. These blips, beeps and static are still in the analysis phase of our investigations. Some have proven to be natural in origin, others may possibly be reflections of our own making and still more very questionable. There have been very few with apparent intelligent patterns that we have yet to decipher."

"Do we have anything emanating from 1826?" asked Kearsay.

"No, General," replied Loehr, "Nothing."

"Intelligent life," said Kearsay to the crowd. "It's apparent we have been visited by some form of intelligent life and we must prepare for whatever may come next." He looked at Bennay, "Professor Loehr, I would ask you to increase your efforts to find some means of communicating with our visitors."

"We have already acted so," returned Loehr, "we're looking at music, numbers and colors as well as spoken words, both here and on the surface."

"Sir," interjected Sarah Hansby, "Professor Loehr and I spoke shortly before this session, and we are pulling together more resources here on the surface to address this problem."

"Thank you, Colonel," returned Kearsay.

As the crowd noise increased, the main view screen flickered alive, "General Kearsay," boomed a deep commanding voice.

"Yes sir, Mister President," replied Kearsay.

Jacob Carsteen's image appeared on screen, "This is a worldwide security issue, and as such, we must involve all the nations of Earth. I will contact Magnas De'Healarm. As the Secretary General of the United Nations, he will undoubtedly call an emergency meeting of the Security Council and another of the general membership. Until then, we should maintain a high alert status and sharpen our swords. General, please contact all SW units and our Lunar and Martian bases. Bring all unnecessary personnel back as close to the surface as we can and be sure all stations and bases are fully armed and prepared for any possible scenario."

"Yes, sir," replied General Kearsay, "this session is being transmitted to all stations. It will take a few hours to converse with SW-13 out near Saturn and longer to bring people in closer.

The view screen went blank and Kearsay said, "Major, a full view of the point of entry."

"Yes sir," said Tetra as she brought up a view of the Kuiper Belt where DD-1826 was first observed.

"Professor Loehr,' said Kearsay, "you were about to say."

"Thank you, General," said Loehr. "So, as the Perdone Galaxy approaches us, we must be aware that any intelligent life existent therein might very well be our equal or better in the several sciences that give us the observation and analytical capabilities we currently possess. Just as we probe the space beyond Kuiper, Oort and out to the full extent of our galactic arm, so too would they in their galaxy." Loehr stepped into the aisle and moved toward the podium, "If I may, General."

Kearsay nodded to Harmon as she pocketed the towel, entered few commands on the control panel and stepped aside, allowing Bennay Loehr access to the microphone. The view screen behind the speaker's podium changed to show an image of the Milky Way. "Our system is here," said Loehr, as he used a laser pointer to indicate one of the main spiral arms of the galaxy. Tetra then zoomed in on the Orion Cygnus's arm in which our solar system exists. "We are here," said Loehr as his laser placed a red dot on the screen, "and here is the arm of Perdone that has begun to mesh with our arm of the Milky Way." He turned to the audience and noted several people entering the room. He nodded and gestured toward open seats, "We have very little information on Perdone, but we have been tracking the nearest of their stars and systems." He looked across the crowd and continued, "There are several potential catastrophic events in the making. Understand that anything we observe today happened about twenty years ago. By now, any number of collisions may have occurred and there are many more that we feel are inevitable. The several planets in this arm," he said as he directed his laser, "appear to be in serious danger in the next few hundred years. We'll refine those calculations as time allows. We see a near definite collision between the fourth planet in the Perdone System, P47-A3- SS-2-M4, and a very heavy asteroid belt around this star," as he placed the laser on another star in their own galactic arm. "The Perdone planet will almost certainly be destroyed or at least seriously damaged and the aftermath is for now very unpredictable. We assume this system—our system, will survive, at least for a millennium, but nothing is certain at this juncture."

Kearsay nodded, "And where does this scenario leave us?"

"Our calculations indicate the first catastrophic event will occur in less than five-hundred years," said Loehr, "depending on a number of factors, like gravitational effects of the two galactic arms approaching one another and other collisions that may have occurred or are now occurring."

"After any large collision, there will be debris everywhere. What are our chances of our being hit?" Kearsay questioned.

"No guarantees, General," returned Loehr, "again, our calculations indicate the collision will occur well outside our solar system and we're confident we will be out of the path of the majority of the planetary debris."

Loehr again tapped the keyboard and turned to the audience as a flight path took shape on the screen. "What you are seeing here in blue is the known flight path of DD-1826 since we noticed it four months ago moving at some ridiculous speed. The yellow is the path we projected as it approached our solar system. It should have passed through well above K Level … M or N, but its speed and course varied, bringing it closer to the Earth. So, we asked that one of your vessels take a closer look. Then it did the unexpected, it made another radical adjustment, diving closer to the Earth's surface. Your pilot tracked DD-1826 as far as he could."

"I couldn't follow it into the upper atmosphere, I'd have burned up," said Darce.

"Yeah, Captain," said Kearsay, "that's why you were called in." He looked back to Loehr, "Lunar base station Alpha has been alerted and they've dispatched a squadron of tactical birds to find and track DD-1826 as it moves away. Their range into space is limited and the Martian orbit bases are also alerted. We've got over 20 units out there looking for this smart rock."

Loehr looked at the view screen and continued, "The red path is from its last observed location and the dashed red is the anticipated return to its own galaxy," he pointed to the fourth planet from a star in the Perdone Galaxy.

Kearsay looked to Loehr, "Tell them the rest."

Loehr touched the keyboard again, the screen zoomed into a system at the very edge of the Perdone Galaxy. He tapped again, and the screen focused on a planet. "This is P47-A3-SS-2-M5. It's not very big, about the size of Earth and it has a gravitational field and atmosphere similar to ours. It's also in line for destruction, a few years ahead of SS-2-M4, but in that it is significantly closer to us, it is of greater interest today. M4 is larger than M5 by about half and will also be of great concern after the destruction of M5."

Darce looked at Jason, "Looks like my port and your storm are on hold for another day or two."

"At least," said Jason.

*   *   *

THREE

2245.08.13.09.43 (Zulu)   Aboard SW-27

General Kearsay's communicator beeped, "General, Stacker here, we have word from a Martian station Sigma tach bird," he said. "DD-1826 is traveling at 1.17 LS-4, they'll keep it in sight as long as possible, but they can't stay with it very long at that speed."

"Projections?" quizzed Kearsay.

"Copy that," returned the Sigma team leader. "We've sent spotters out ahead of DD-1826's calculated path, as far as they can reach 'til it gets there and passes them."

"The Hawking is out near the Jupiter orbit," said Kearsay, "their tach birds are close enough to intercept 1826 and track it."

"General, we have three probes out over the Kuiper Belt, EXP-23 is within range of DD-1826's path. Should I re-task and move closer?"

"Yeah," returned Kearsay. "If the equipment on board is still in working order, and we have enough time to reposition, we may be able to scan for power surges or additional gravitational fluctuations."

Hansby chimed in, "1826 is picking up speed. We won't be able to catch up or reposition anything in time to improve readings."

"What's her speed now?" quizzed Kearsay.

"It's over 2.2 LS-4, and still accelerating," returned Hansby.

"A visit from something alien," said Kearsay. "What should we expect next?" He walked back toward his office, "Major, assemble the senior staff in the large conference room and get me an open line to the president."

"Aye, sir," replied Tetra.

*   *   *

2245.08.13.11.05 (Zulu) Aboard SW-27—Main Conference Room

Bennay Loehr stood, "General, we have all heard stories of aliens visiting Earth and seen countless science-fiction movies about invasions and monsters, but never substantiated. The events of today have been a confirmation of something, or someone, out there with the capability of reaching our planet. Just what their intentions are remains to be seen. We should be prepared for any of the numerous possibilities."

"Understood, Professor Loehr," said Kearsay. "What do you consider a likely scenario?"

"We have examined the flight path of the object 1826 and made several assumptions," said Eunice Carlon. "The object was not seen until it was coming through the Kuiper belt. The explanations are few—we completely missed it in previous viewings. It has some sort of cloaking capability, or it was moving at LS-0 or greater prior to entering the Kuiper."

"Based on those possibilities, any further thoughts?" asked Loehr.

"First, we've been watching that portion of the sky for at least two years," said Carlon. "The Perdone moving into this arm of our galaxy has a high probability of altering the flight paths of many objects and we want to be prepared to deal with any potential catastrophic event. Even with our increased attention to that sector, including a review of prior scans, we've not seen anything on the order of 1826 so, we've ruled that out."

"Second?" asked Kearsay.

"The next possibility is the capability to hide an object through a cloaking mechanism," said Carlon. "Why would they have turned it off at the Kuiper belt?" She looked around the room and continued, "Thus we tend to eliminate that possibility."

"And third?" asked Loehr, looking at Carlon.

"Third," responded Carlon, "the possibility that 1826 was moving at the LS-0 level or greater. As it was moving away from our planet, it increased speed and finally disappeared, as you would expect if it reached light speed. We have trained our sensors on the estimated flight path of 1826, and if we are correct, it would appear as the light traveled back."

"Any results?" asked Kearsay.

"Yes, General," replied Carlon, "we have a few blurred images which indicate a very fast-moving object exactly where 1826 would be on its way back to the Perdone."

Bennay Loehr rose again, "General, the object traveled at some phenomenal speed, scanned our planet, and is probably heading back to its point of origin. They are obviously ahead of us in one or two areas and maybe more. If these beings are in any way aggressive and see us as several links down the food chain ... we could have a real problem."

"Understood," said Kearsay. "What could they want?"

"If I may, General," said Carlon, "the Perdone is some twenty light-years away. We are seeing now what happened twenty years ago at that distance and we can predict what may happen in the next few hundred years. Several of the planets in one arm of their spiral will likely be destroyed. Any civilization there would be inspired to search for another secure world which they could inhabit ... alongside the current residents, or instead of." She paused, "I know if it were our world threatened with destruction, I'd be looking for a new address and if I found only one, I'd think of my people before considering the welfare of others."

"Are you suggesting they may try to conquer the Earth?"

"I think it is a real possibility that we must consider," returned Carlon, "so, yes General, I am."

* * *

2245.08.14.13.37 (Zulu) Earth, North American Presidents Offices

The President conferred with Mangnas De'Healarm and an immediate security council meeting was arranged at the UN Headquarters in New York. The meeting was brief, Mangnas reported on the encounter and several nations returned with statements about an unknown object passing overhead and disappearing.

Mangnas then made a suggestion, "Let's all take the next three days to digest this information and consult with our individual teams. We can reassemble on the 17th, then hopefully we're able to determine what we should or could do to be prepared for whatever happens next."

2245.08.17.15.12 (Zulu) Earth, UN Headquarters

The event caused panic in some quarters and hope in others. Contact with an alien species had been the thing of science fiction books and movies for three-hundred years. Periodic UFO sightings or claims of being taken prisoners aboard a spacecraft, along with speculations about crop circles and cave paintings, had generated a plethora of possible scenarios.

"We don't know who or what this may lead to," said Mangnas as he addressed the assembled nation representatives. "I am reminded that any intelligent life forms existent in this universe could well be our equal or exceed us in intelligence. I propose we hope for the best and prepare for the worst."

The multiple military organizations on Earth agreed that any alien force aggressively approaching the planet would not single out a specific nation. Any attack would be against the entire globe and thus it behooved them to cooperate in a coordinated response.

Space-capable fighter craft were checked and prepared for combat. Each multi-tiered, rotating space station was provided with four tach birds for each operating ring and two crews for each bird. The birds were equipped with two-hundred-kilowatt laser cannons and four missiles with two-hundred-kilogram warheads. In addition, each station's central column was equipped with one-megawatt laser cannon and eight small missiles with five-hundred-kilogram warheads.

The activity aboard the stations intensified as the crews practiced launching the tach birds, maneuvering around the station, and returning. Missiles had not been needed in great numbers as the threat of asteroids approaching the rotating space stations or Earth had drastically reduced in the last hundred years. The current supplies were checked, and new missiles were ordered. The supply held on the planet was quickly dispersed and emergency manufacture orders were placed.

It was practice and hope as the days passed. Days turned to weeks and the level of tension lessened as nothing new was detected approaching Earth.

Practice sessions at the space stations were reduced and life almost returned to normal.

* * *

FOUR

2245.11.09.12.14 (Zulu)   Aboard SW-27

Major Harmon entered General Kearsay's office, again covered in grease and dirt, wiping her hands nervously.

"Still working on that old tach bird, Major?" asked Kearsay as he noticed her level of tension.

"Yes sir," she replied. "Might even get it to fly again."

"Good luck with that," he returned. "So, what's happening?"

She cleared her throat and responded, "Sir, it appears we have another object heading this way, but this one is different than 1826."

"Another smart rock?" asked Kearsay.

"No sir, it has very definite smooth lines and has made at least two course adjustments. It appears to be a large, controlled vessel."

"It's not one of ours?" questioned Kearsay.

"No sir, we've checked all our vessels and our allies," said Tetra. "We first saw it a few minutes ago as it came out of the Kuiper Belt."

"Raise the current alert status," said Kearsay.

"Already in motion," said Tetra. She hesitated as her com-link stirred. "Excuse me, sir, another message," she said as she answered the call. She looked confused as she said, "It just shed six smaller vessels," she paused, "they have adopted a 'V' formation."

"And?" demanded Kearsay.

"They appear to have structure, instrumentation, and most likely, occupants."

"We're just seeing it now?" quizzed Kearsay.

"Yes sir," returned Tetra.

"So, once again, it was either moving more than LS-0," said Kearsay, "or, they have a cloaking capability?"

"Yes sir," said Tetra.

"Are Loehr and Carlon still on board?" asked Kearsay.

"Not sure sir," replied Tetra.

"If they're not ..." started Kearsay.

"I'll find them sir, and make sure they're on board," returned Tetra.

"Thank you, Major," Kearsay pondered the possibilities for a moment. "How many occupants?"

"Don't know sir, I would guess one or two in the smaller craft and probably more in the larger vessel," said Tetra.

"What kind of occupants?"

"Sensors can't tell from this distance," returned Tetra. "We may get a better reading when they're closer."

"You're sure this isn't one of ours?" wondered Kearsay aloud.

"We checked and nobody has been out beyond Kuiper," replied Tetra. "And we've never seen a vessel with this configuration."

"Any communication?" queried Kearsay.

"No, nothing yet," returned Harmon. "We've opened a few channels, trying to make contact."

"Could they be military—attacking us?"

"Don't know," said Tetra, "we've alerted the other stations and Ground Control. Tach bird teams and their ships are being rechecked as we speak and along with the increased alert status, I've taken the liberty of ordering four birds out."

"Very good, Major. How much time do we have?"

"At their current speed, a hundred hours," returned Harmon. "They just passed through the Kuiper, and probably slowed down to navigate."

Harmon's com-link lit up, she looked at Kearsay, "Sir, we're getting a transmission. Based on the distance, they would have transmitted about four hours ago. So, they sent it while still in the Kuiper."

"What are they saying?"

Harmon mumbled something into her com-link, then looked at Kearsay, "They said 'hello', in English sir. They speak English."

"Have we responded?"

"No sir, this just came in."

"Anybody else respond?"

Major Harmon repeated the question into her com-link, "They're checking."

"Okay, assemble the team in the briefing room. I have to call the president."

"Aye sir, and I'll clean up and join the meeting."

* * *

Twenty minutes later, Kearsay and Harmon entered the briefing room. Harmon now in uniform, no longer looked like a mechanic. She was a tall, athletic-looking woman, with close-cut brown hair and piercing blue eyes, which were now directed at the general, "Sir, are you ready to begin?"

"Yes Major, main screen, please," said Kearsay.

"Aye sir," replied Harmon.

The main screen came on and Kearsay entered a few commands. A view of SW-27 on one half of the screen and the president on the other.

"Mr. President," said Kearsay, "you're on screen."

"Thank you, General," said President Jacob Carsteen. "Ladies and gentlemen, we are being approached by an unknown entity. We must proceed carefully. Please do not respond or react in any way to their transmissions. We'll handle that here."

As he was speaking the half screen of SW-27 changed to a deep space view.

"Major, what do we have?" enquired Kearsay.

"Another transmission and it appears some visuals," returned Harmon.

"Are you putting them on screen?" asked Kearsay.

"Trying, sir," said Harmon. "Kind of like television signals from a century ago."

As she was speaking the screen flickered and showed a view of space. A view looking at the earth from the Kuiper Belt.

"We are approaching your station SW-27," said a humanlike voice. "Arrival estimated in two of your hours."

The president spoke immediately, "We would like to welcome you. Will you come to the planet's surface?"

Fifteen minutes passed, and another signal arrived, this time with an accompanying video of two human-like figures standing in a shadowy room. One of the figures stepped forward into the light. The figure was much like a man in build; two arms, two legs, and a head attached to a torso. The being's height could not be determined but its skin was a grey-green hue with dark eyes slightly larger than a human's and round in shape. Its arms were long, ending in hands with human-like fingers. Its head was free of hair. The ears, nose and mouth were much like that of a human. It was dressed in a high-collared, navy-blue jacket that fell to its hips. "I am an envoy, come to negotiate a peaceful meeting of our leaders to discuss certain accommodations."

"You speak our language?" said Kearsay.

"Yes, we have observed your radio and television transmissions for years. We're aware of a number of languages used across your planet. We have studied the transmissions for a long time and have chosen the English language because of its use in so many of the transmissions we have received."

The president spoke, "I am Jacob Carsteen, President of the North American United Nations. May I ask your name?"

"Mr. President, my name might be very difficult to pronounce, but it most closely resembles Marshall. Please call me Marshall."

"Very well, Marshall. Will you be coming to the planet's surface?"

"As you undoubtedly noted, I am aboard the larger of our vessels, it is a command ship, the Karnis Tarb and carries six war craft, Tarb Cains. These Cains are here with me for my protection and "I have been instructed not to descend to the planet's surface. All conversation will occur at your SW-27. I will advise you when my Shom, my shuttle, will be ready to leave the Karnis."

"I will try to be there when you arrive," said Carsteen.

* * *

General Kearsay called Major Harmon into his office and ordered a complete survey and cleaning of SW-27. "It's not like Mom or Uncle Bob is coming to dinner. This is as big as it gets, for now." As Harmon was leaving Kearsay's office he added, "Major, I don't want people staring like they're at the zoo. This is very important. We treat these beings as if they are part of our daily routine—no gawking, no staring, no comments. Understood?"

"Aye sir," replied Major Harmon, "we should also prepare the landing pad in Maintenance Bay 'A' for their arrival."

"See to it, Major," said Kearsay.

* * *

FIVE

2245.11.10.13.17 (Zulu)   Aboard SW 27

Carsteen's presidential shuttle arrived as the seven alien craft approached SW-27.

The maintenance bay control officer opened a channel to the president's shuttle, "Shuttle SS-01 please align with portal B-2, middle ring. The docking collar lights are on, and the clamps are ready to accept your shuttle."

"Copy that," returned the shuttle pilot. The four main clamps reached down and connected with the shuttle, "We have you connected, SS-01."

"Copy that," returned the shuttle pilot, "releasing to your control."

The shuttle was drawn to the docking collar, secured and an elevator was lowered through the docking collar.

President Carsteen and his team were lifted into the maintenance bay. The new arrivals were met by General Kearsay, "Welcome aboard, Mr. President."

"Thank you, General," said Carsteen. "Please see to it that my aide, Colonel Bracken is given access to all communications and anything else he needs."

Kearsay extended his hand, "Colonel."

"Jim Bracken, sir," replied the aide.

Kearsay waved over a technician, "Sergeant, take the Colonel to the empty office next to mine and see to it he has anything he needs."

"Aye, sir," responded the Sergeant as he extended his hand toward a door, "this way sir."

Carsteen then said, "I need a space to contact Marshall."

"My office," responded Kearsay. "This way sir," he led the president to his office.

"Sir," said Kearsay, "the alien ship, the Karnis and its Cains are currently holding a position three kilometers from this station. They're awaiting an invitation to come aboard."

"Give me a few minutes to get my thoughts together and talk to Colonel Bracken," said Carsteen. "We should only need another minute to be fully prepped."

"Sir, Colonel Bracken is in the next office," Kearsay said.

Two minutes later Bracken asked Kearsay to join them for the call to the Karnis. Kearsay opened a channel and hailed the Karnis. Immediately another transmission was received aboard SW-27. "We have arrived and are prepared to come aboard your station," said Marshall.

General Kearsay responded, "We are ready for your arrival. The atmosphere aboard this station is similar to conditions on the planet's surface. We trust you are aware of those conditions and ask if any special accommodations are necessary?"

Marshall returned, "Thank you for asking. We are aware of the conditions aboard your station and believe no special accommodations are necessary. We will be leaving the Karnis now."

Kearsay looked out a small portal and saw several lights move away from the Karnis Tarb and move cautiously toward SW-27. The maintenance bay officer had full communication with the Shom and directed the pilot toward the maintenance bay doors in the 'A' ring. When the Shom was finally positioned, a pair of doors opened horizontally, and a second pair of doors opened vertically. The space inside the two sets of doors was just big enough for the Shom to fit inside. As the Shom set down on the deck, the two sets of doors closed, and air was introduced into the area. Then the interior doors opened and the Shom was maneuvered into the larger maintenance bay.

Marshall and three slightly larger figures dressed in dark green tunics, similar to Marshall's blue uniform, exited the shuttle. Each of the three carried a meter-long hollow tube with a thicker band at one end and a wrist band that matched. The tubes were treated as if they were weapons. Marshall paused just outside the Shom, inhaled, sampling the air, then turned and looked toward an opening door. He waited and watched.

An unarmed guard of twenty men created a path from the Shom to the door out of the bay. President Carsteen came through the door and met Marshall halfway to the shuttle. He was slightly taller than Carsteen, still less than two meters in height. Carsteen extended a hand and Marshall met him with an open hand. "It is my pleasure to welcome you to this station and look forward to our conversation," said Carsteen.

Marshall looked about the bay, at the guards, the three people accompanying the president and finally, his eyes rested on Carsteen. He gestured toward the three beings behind him, each about an even two meters in height and heavily muscled. "These are my guards. They will remain with me throughout my visit here. I trust you find that acceptable."

"While not necessary, they are welcome as well," responded Carsteen. "May I introduce General Kearsay, Colonel Bracken and Major Harmon."

Marshall acknowledged the three and again looked about the maintenance bay, "Our latest information on your planet carried very little on your recent technological developments. I find all of this very interesting. The last probe we sent was intended to update our records and learn of your most recent technological advancements, but you have secured much of your military information in files we have not yet been able to access."

A nod from Carsteen to Kearsay and a glance from the general to Major Harmon and she quietly spoke into her com-link, "Stand easy, weapons holstered." The reaction was an immediate breath of relief. This was not to be a conflict situation.

"We were unaware of your existence until recently," said Carsteen "there is much to talk about, and we now welcome you. Please come this way." He led Marshall into the station interior to a large conference room, "Please sit and we may continue our conversation."

Marshall looked about the room and replied, "These chairs would be rather uncomfortable, if I may ask, could I use one of those crates?" He gestured toward several shipping containers.

Two staffers immediately moved a container to the conference table. Marshall thanked them and sat. The three guards who accompanied him stood at his back and appeared to relax. Their tubes were moved to their backs, and they scanned the room, their eyes resting on each individual for a few seconds.

"First," said Carsteen, "may I offer you any refreshments?"

"No," returned Marshall, "we are still in the process of checking your various water supplies to determine which best suits us. Your filtering processes seem to produce the best results and the several chemical treatments employed at major water treatment facilities are still being evaluated. So, we have brought our own supply."

"Your guards, do they also speak our language?" asked Carsteen.

"Yes, it was a requirement," said Marshall. "We have established teams of our people who have visited numerous worlds, each has a language and various customs the team must learn. The crews of the Karnis and the Cains may be referred to as a part of the Earth team. All members of this team had to be fluent in a common Earth language."

"We seem to have many similar features," said Carsteen. "It raises the question—are we somehow connected?"

"Yes," returned Marshall, "we have a common ancestor."

Carsteen puzzled for a moment, "Can you elaborate?"

"Yes, to a degree," began Marshall. "This universe as you see it and by your calculations, came into existence approximately thirteen-billion of your years ago as you measure time. The several theories about the beginning of the universe, including the Big Bang, do not necessarily recognize the existence of anything prior to that event. We have also concluded that there was such an occurrence, but we have gone deeper. All of this we see, did not just appear. It existed somewhere else in the form of energy or matter. Some of the energy and material came from other universes that may have had their time billions or trillions of your years ago, or even longer.

"That included everything from stars, planets, asteroids and the several gases, all the way down to the atomic and sub-atomic levels. All from countless Big Bang-type events, the collisions of two or more universes, or the collisions of several dimensions. Each ending of a star, a galaxy or an entire universe and the subsequent disbursement of its elements did not necessarily rip everything down to is smallest parts. Many elements may well have survived a collapse and re-expansion processes, thus becoming parts of the new stars and planets in this, as well as other new universes.

"How arrogant we both have been in our histories to believe that we existed alone in the only universe that ever existed. Our development has been observed, as has yours, by a race of beings who may have seeded our planet with the basics of life. Life that has included a continuation of their race in numerous forms and in as many places as they could reach."

Marshall paused and noticed rapt attention from his hosts, he continued. "At some point, we don't know when, where or how, the galaxies we see here in this universe were visited by that race of beings who seeded various planets in a great number of galaxies with different elements and the numerous strings of DNA that they perceived would guarantee the continuation of life. We have no idea how many seeds were sewn, undoubtedly more, many more than have survived. Our explorations have identified more than fifteen-hundred worlds in the small portion of this universe we have been able to visit, where life does exist in some form. Life where the DNA which we have been able to collect over time, conclusively demonstrates that we, both your people and ours are sufficiently similar to assume we are rooted in a common ancestor."

"So, these beings planted DNA and allowed it to develop?" queried Carsteen.

"We don't know the exact process, but we surmise as any good farmer, the planters tended their crops. They may have been the originators of life streams in some cases, donors in some, and simply observers in others. Our planet has been visited many times over the millions or billions of years since the seeding."

"Who are these beings?" asked Carsteen.

"As I said, they have been doing this seeding for a very long time. We have no idea who the originators were or are. We know the beings who visit our planet and probably this planet of yours are called the Talmonoria. They may be the originators, or some other race springing from the originators, continuing the work of the original planters."

"The Talmonoria," said Carsteen with a hint of wonder. "So, do we resemble these ancestors?" he inquired.

Marshall paused thoughtfully, "The seeds with varying DNA structures scattered throughout the several universes have led to many species, each developing in different gravitational and atmospheric conditions thus leading to a countless number of species in as many shapes and sizes as you can imagine. Your dinosaurs, for instance, were not uncommon, and similar creatures are still found in different worlds."

"Understood," returned Carsteen, "but how closely do we resemble the Talmonoria?"

"In many ways, we both do, but we probably resemble each other more than either of us resemble the farmers. The many features we share include the brain, functioning at a level well below its fully developed capacity, complex communication capability, dexterous physical capability, along with the physical size and strength to rise to the top of our respective food chains," replied Marshall.

"Fully developed capacity?" puzzled Carsteen.

"It varies—but, yes," returned Marshall, "we speculate the Talmonoria have gone far beyond whatever levels we may have achieved. Perhaps as much as we are above a tree, they are above us both."

"So, all seeded planets are developing as we have here, and you have on your home planet?" quizzed Carsteen.

"No," replied Marshall, "there are undoubtedly many more failures than successes and there are even more that are still in a primitive stage of development, just as this Earth was only a few million years ago."

Carsteen thought for a moment then, "Are the Talmonoria still out there?"

Marshall nodded, "Most definitely, yes. They have visited our planet many times recently and even confirmed to us that our two galaxies were going to collide."

Again, Carsteen paused, "And have they been here, on Earth?"

"Yes, absolutely," replied Marshall with a nod. "We have limited communication with them, only when they visit and those visits are brief and years apart, but we have had very informative conversations."

“Visits?” echoed Carsteen.

“Yes, they come periodically to check on development, take some samples of various lifeforms and sometimes introduce or remove something.”

“So, have they helped in your technological development?” asked Carsteen.

“No, not really. For the most part, they insist we learn and grow on our own, the information about the collision of our galaxies was more a confirmation of our observations and suspicions. Our developments in space travel, working with different forms of energy, have both been mostly of our own making.”

“Different forms of energy,” returned Carsteen. “We’d appreciate some assistance in that area.”

“Yes, of course,” said Marshall. “It would be most advantageous here on Earth. Collection and storage of the elements of energy is a slow and tedious process. Once collected and in sufficient quantity, this energy can power a planet’s industry as well as travel without harming the other elements of life. It has been in use on our home planet for more than 300 of our years. We have one older facility located on our home planet that has been in operation for most of that time and another, space-based facility recently brought on-line located in orbit about a nearby planet.”

“So, you are able to easily wander the universe,” said Carsteen.

“Not exactly, each space vessel making a significant voyage to your planet or many of the other planets we have investigated like Earth, has been a significant drain on our reserves. The new facility has allowed more travel. We continue to collect energy and would consider establishing a new collection and storage facility here in orbit about Earth or your moon.”

“Could it be built on Earth’s surface?” asked Carsteen.

“The logistics of where and what systems and processes would be used would be decisions made by our scientists and engineers,” returned Marshall.

“Understand that for years, we burned fossil fuels as an energy source,” said Carsteen, “then developed nuclear capability and after that, solar, wind, tidal, but we still burn oil and gas in limited quantities.”

"Yes, we know," returned Marshall. "The energy we capture and use, would replace all your current sources and have no negative effect on air quality. The greatest hurdle would be building the collection and storage facility, then collecting enough energy to operate the facility and finally deliver the excess energy to the planet's surface. I believe this process could take twenty to thirty of your years from beginning construction to delivery of substantial power."

"Twenty or thirty years is a long time," returned Carsteen.

"It is," said Marshall, "I am a diplomat, not a scientist, but my understanding is when the first space-based facility is on-line, a second station could be built in about half the time and at much less cost."

"Could we bring in our engineers and scientists to learn more about this energy collection process?" asked Carsteen.

"Again," returned Marshall, "this is not my area of expertise, and my objective here today is to arrange a meeting of our leaders wherein many of your questions may be asked and answered."

Carsteen did not wish to offend the alien and therefore changed the subject, "And what of the Talmonoria's involvement, would they be involved in any of this?" asked Carsteen.

"I cannot speak for them," said Marshall, they visit us periodically, often without warning and usually maintain a distance, not helping or guiding our efforts. We believe their purpose is to spread intelligent life into as many places as they can. Intelligent life that springs from their DNA."

"So, where are they?"

"We don't know, they may be here now, and we may never know."

"What about their home world, have you ever visited them? Does it still exist?"

"The original planet?" returned Marshall, "I have no idea. I think they have established colonies countless times, and may have moved their own base world, always looking for another long-time situation and many of the past planets of occupation are still there, just as many are gone." Marshall looked about the room gauging the reactions of listeners. "They are now on multiple planets in countless galaxies and at as many levels of development. Understand, we have no idea how old this race of beings is. They may have been in existence billions or trillions of years ago, or more here in this universe or some other universe. We simply don't know."

Carsteen wondered aloud, "Just how advanced are they?"

Marshall leaned forward, "You must understand, they have seeded many planets and galaxies. There are uncountable colonies as well as newly established life beginnings. We can only assume there are as many more advanced than us as there are less advanced. We feel our situation, as yours, is somewhere in the middle, then again, we may still be considered primitive, we just don't know. There are planets with numerous lifeforms, similar to those that do or have existed here on your Earth, some more advanced and some less."

"Are the inhabitants of those planets like us?" asked Carsteen, "Able to communicate and coexist?"

"We have visited more than 1,500 planets where life has been detected," said Marshall. "Some, very few, are very much like us. Most are different but still connected, and there are many where the life process has had radically different results."

"How advanced are these farmers of life?" asked Carsteen. "And how close are we to them?"

"We know very little of the numerous others they have seeded, we do know some have developed very rapidly and are far ahead of us. Some may have even surpassed the farmers themselves. That we don't know. As far as our development, they are still significantly ahead of our level, but we are getting closer with the passing of time."

Carsteen said, "We've still never gotten an indication of your energy capabilities and wonder at your travel capabilities."

"That is not a topic we will discuss, as I have said, I am a diplomat, not a scientist," said Marshall. "I can tell you this, we have been able to identify and function in several dimensions above those known to and used by your people."

"Several dimensions?" puzzled Carsteen.

"Yes," returned Marshall, "these assist in our transportation and communication."

"Will your scientists tell us about that?" asked Major Harmon.

"Perhaps," replied Marshall.

"Exactly what will be the topic of our conversation," asked Carsteen.

"Our planet is destined for destruction," said Marshall. "We will collide with another body in 342 of our years; that is close to 512 years on your planet. Our days are longer than yours, approximately 32 of your hours and the time to complete one revolution about our star takes 410 of our days."

"What do you call your planet?" asked Carsteen.

"Again, probably very difficult to pronounce in your language," said Marshall, "but you may say Dar'Wan."

"We have referred to your home as P47-A3- SS-2-M4," said Carsteen. "Dar'Wan is much easier to say and you're certain of this time … 512 years by our count?"

"Yes, the calculations by numerous scientists have given the same result," said Marshall.

"We have also noted another endangered planet," said Carsteen, "we have designated it as P47-A3- SS-2-M5."

"You refer to Dar'Fost, a planet we have used as a place for criminals, energy storage and scientific experimentation," returned Marshall, "yes, it too will be destroyed." He paused and continued, "My mission here is to arrange a meeting of our leaders with your leaders to determine a course of action which will find and perhaps develop new worlds for us both to continue, much like our ancestors have done over time from the beginning."

Carsteen returned, "We would welcome your leaders here or on the planet's surface for meetings and discussion."

Marshall added, "We also suggest a meeting of the scientific communities of both worlds."

"Are your people involved in religion?" asked Carsteen.

"Yes," said Marshall, "we have several religious groups who have all asked to be involved in discussions."

"So, you believe in God?" quizzed Carsteen.

"Some of our religions follow a similar path as your theory of a prime mover, an uncaused-cause, and these theories have many followers, but none are an official belief of the governing body. Our people believe whatever they wish."

"What about an afterlife?" asked Carsteen, "Heaven and hell."

"Many do believe in those concepts," said Marshall. "There are various theories. Most believe there is an inner being with all life forms, a being which you call a soul or a spirit. This spirit lives on in another dimension after your physical body has ceased to function."

"Another dimension?" puzzled Carsteen.

"More likely another series of dimensions which do not recognize our concept of time or distance," said Marshall. "Some go further and believe as a spirit moves from our world to these new or different dimensions, it may exist in some higher form or become a part of a great singular being. A great spirit."

"This is what you believe?" asked Carsteen.

Marshall hesitated then said, "I am not religious and believe the end of life as we know it is the end, there is nothing else."

Carsteen realized that topic was not to be carried further, looked at Marshall and with great caution, said, "And military?"

"Yes, at some point we will introduce our military leaders," said Marshall, "that will likely occur much later." He gestured toward the three guards, "These three individuals are from our military forces and will accompany me, as others will and have also traveled with our other diplomats."

"Now, we have to determine the when, where, and who for our next meeting," said Carsteen.

"Yes, our highest leader, similar to Mangnas De'Healarm, the Secretary General of your United Nations wants to personally be involved," returned Marshall. "Would he, Mangnas, be amenable to that?"

"I cannot speak for him, but I believe he will be most anxious for such a meeting. He's already been contacted and made aware of this visit and would have been here if possible."

"We suggest the inclusion of all Nations Presidents or leaders," said Marshall.

"Yes, by all means. Now, the when and where," said Carsteen. "We do not have the travel capability as you do, I suggest we assemble on the planet's surface at our United Nations headquarters."

"Yes, I understand, but we believe the initial few sessions should occur here in this station, SW-27 and on one of our vessels, the Karnis Tarb," said Marshall as he stood.

The three guards moved to allow Marshall to turn and face the assembled crowd in the room. "We will return to our vessel now and allow you to make arrangements for these meetings. We may reconvene in 10 of your days, or more, if you need the time."

"Then may we expect you will be accompanied by your leaders?" asked Carsteen.

"I will communicate with them as soon as I return to our vessel, it may take several of your days to confirm the arrangements and transport the proper individuals to this location. I will let you know as soon as I know," said Marshall. "Thank you for allowing this session. I will return to my vessel and begin the next step in this meeting." The session ended and Marshall returned to his Shom and flew back to the Karnis Tarb.

* * *

SIX

2245.11.15.22.28 (Zulu)   Aboard SW 27

The next few days were full of activity, getting the large conference room ready for the upcoming meetings. Accommodations were made for twenty-four Earth leaders and the visiting aliens. Their support teams were limited to six people each. Carsteen and Bracken had prepared their presentation and rehearsed it as much as needed. "We're ready for anything," said Carsteen. "You go get some rest, Colonel. When this starts, it could go on for a while."

"Thank you, sir, are you sure there's nothing else?" asked Colonel Bracken.

"I think we've covered all the bases," said Carsteen, "this is more De'Healarm's show, we're the 'B' team, just backup."

*   *   *

Darce had requested a tach bird from SW-27. His assigned bird was tied to SW-23 and the backup crew had already assumed command. He hoped SW-27 could provide them with a newer model bird and was waiting for an answer.

Jason spent most of his free time working out, staying in shape and he found SW-27's gym with enough equipment to occupy him for several hours. Darce wondered about the view from SW-27's observation deck in the central core. He wandered up to an observation deck, found a comfortable chair and leaned back looking out at the stars. He took a ride on a lift to the core and another lift to the observation deck. He found a comfortable bench, strapped himself in, and was wondering if there was a star in that great cosmos that may have a planet where some other soul could be looking in the direction of Earth. A view that could be hundreds or thousands of years crossing the universe.

Major Harmon had halted work on the old tach bird and cleaned and stowed all her tools in preparation for the arrival of the aliens. She dressed in her class A uniform and was ready to engage with the influx of national leaders from Earth and the aliens. "Anything else before we are visited?" she asked Kearsay.

"Not that I can see," returned the General. "You can't do any more work on your project ..."

"The Blue Wolf," she replied. "It's an older model tach bird, just needs a few more adjustments and I'd like to take it for a spin around the moon." She looked out the portal, "It's been fun learning about the older systems." She turned and looked at the General, "I can't work on my pet project 'til this has settled down, so I'm going to wander up to the observation deck and look at the stars."

The area was dark, and Tetra saw a figure relaxed on a bench. Holding on to grab bars, she crossed the room. "Sleeping on the job, Captain?"

"Ah, welcome to my private office," returned Darce. She was no longer the grease-covered mechanic fussing over an old tach bird in the maintenance bay. *Whoa ... she scrubs up damn nice.* He paused and almost stammered, "A great place to gaze at the stars and wonder about everything and anything from termites to Titans," he said as he continued to look at her.

"And what is your wonder about today?" she asked as she sat on a bench opposite Darce.

"I wonder if someone out there is sitting on a beach watching a sunrise or looking at the stars and wondering as I wonder," he said, "who could be out there, looking at us."

"Just any star or do you have one specific one you watch?" she asked.

Darce was looking past Tetra, "Kinda," he replied. "That one," he said pointing over her left shoulder.

She stood and moved closer to the other bench, "May I join you, Captain?" she asked with a smile.

"Sure, and my name is Darce, Major."

"Tetra," she returned as she sat next to him, "call me Tetra. Now which star are you watching?"

They sat together talking about stars and sunrises for an hour before Darce put his arm around her and gently pulled her closer.

* * *

SEVEN

2245.11.15.23.12 (Zulu)   Aboard SW-27

SW-27 is a three-ring rotating space station, approximately 250 meters in height and 400 meters in diameter. The rings rotate at a perimeter velocity of about 5 meters per second. Each ring has four portals that can accept the connection collars of several types of craft including cargo freighters, tach birds and trash haulers. This outer ring also had a large multi-panel door able to accept any of the haulers, shuttles, or tach birds into an open maintenance bay for repair or maintenance.

Mangnas De'Healarm, the Secretary General of the United Nations of Earth arrived aboard the American President's shuttle. The shuttle was secured at portal number A-3's collar where De'Healarm immediately came aboard and met with Carsteen. As they were speaking other leaders arrived at other portals in the A and C rings and they all assembled in the B-ring's large conference room.

"We must be very aware of the actual intentions of these aliens," said Mangnas to an assembled group. "We know nothing of their objectives or their military capability. They indicated the imminent destruction of their planet will necessitate relocation of their population and this planet; Earth is already at near capacity. We have room for very few and they may be looking for much more."

The conversations between leaders continued over the next four days as they awaited the arrival of the Dar'Wanian leaders. The Karnis Tarb and its six Cains remained in fixed positions around SW-27 approximately three to five kilometers away.

On the fourth day Colonel Hansby contacted Kearsay as he was meeting with Carsteen and De'Healarm. "Sir, a vessel has just come out of the Kuiper, we assume it is the Dar'Wan leaders."

"Have we received any communication?" asked De'Healarm.

"No sir," returned Hansby.

As she was about to continue, her com-link chirped, "Colonel, we have a message from Marshall."

"Copy, put it through to this link," he commanded.

"Aye, sir."

Marshall's voice was easily heard, "Our leader, Tarm'Daak Flamnar has arrived aboard the Enkar Tarb. We may begin our meetings as soon as you are ready."

De'Healarm returned, "Do you need time to prepare for our initial meeting?"

A second voice, deeper and authoritative, spoke in an unknown tongue and Marshall translated, "No, we are ready now." He then added, "We have prepared a room on this vessel. It is ready for our two leaders to meet."

De'Healarm spoke again, "We thought we would have all our leaders involved in this conversation. Can you accept an influx of sixty-three people?"

"No, that would strain our air and power reserves," said Marshall. "An alternative would be a private virtual meeting between the two leaders. Can you arrange that?"

"Yes," returned Mangnas, "I can use General Kearsay's office for the conversation." He went into the large conference room and addressed the assembled world leaders. "Their leader, Tarm'Daak Flamnar wishes to speak to me alone in a secured communication first, then they wish to come aboard SW-27 and we all may join in conversation." He looked about the room and with enough approving nods he turned to Kearsay and said, "General, please join me for a moment in your office."

Mangnas and Kearsay went into the general's office and closed the door, "General, I don't know where this is going to lead, but I suggest you quietly stand by for some military action. I don't like this character's tone. It was too sharp, too commanding and I'm uncomfortable."

"Understood sir," said Kearsay. "I'll make the preparations without sounding an alarm."

"Good, now if you'll excuse me."

Kearsay touched a switch, "Flip this to open the com-link and watch the monitor," he said. "If there are visuals, they'll appear there.'

"Thank you, General," said Mangnas as he flipped the switch.

A large alien figure, dressed in a black tunic appeared on the monitor and could see Mangnas as well, "Mr. Secretary General, I am Tarm'Daak Flamnar," he said in a deep, heavily accented, and rumbling voice.

Marshall then said, "Tarm'Daak is not fluent in your language, so I will translate."

Tarm'Daak spoke again and Marshall translated, "I speak for the Dar'Wannian people."

Mangnas replied, "Welcome to our system, Tarm'Daak Flamnar, I am Mangnas De'Healarm, Secretary General of the United Federation of Earth Nations. I function as an equal to the Earth's leaders and will be pleased to introduce you to them and speak as their representative." He paused as Flamnar seemed to ponder Mangnas' statement and Mangnas continued, "You have come to negotiate an arrangement between our worlds..."

Flamnar forcefully interrupted him and again Marshall translated, "You must understand, this will not be a negotiation. I am here to tell you what we are going to do."

Mangnas looked slightly startled and said, "You may ask anything you wish, but we don't bow to demands of any kind."

Flamnar listened to Marshall's translation and raised his voice in his language, "Some of your leaders on board your SW-27 will argue and wish to resist what I say." The viewer followed Flamnar to a portal looking out toward one of the Dar'Wannian vessels and he continued, "Our planet is going to be destroyed and we need a place to relocate. This planet is one of the few we have identified as possibly acceptable. Of those, this is the closest in size, atmosphere and climate to our home and thus perhaps most capable of accepting our population. All scans thus far have verified this, and we wish to begin the relocation process of our people here and yours to another planet as soon as possible. We will allow you to select from the other planets we have found, or you may seek out other worlds on your own."

As Marshall translated, Mangnas' sense of ire rose and he argued, "Again, Flamnar, this is completely unacceptable."

"We have two transport class vessels ready to begin the relocation process from Dar'Wan," said Marshall and he continued translating, "We will be bringing in teams of our scientists and our military. The scientists will begin the process of developing the water and air treatments and our military will begin by taking control of your defense systems."

Mangnas also raised his voice to a commanding level and replied, "What you're describing is an invasion and that will not be allowed."

Flamnar listened and said to Marshall, "I understand your hesitance in moving, but *you* must understand we have no choice. If we both move simultaneously, it could all work out well." Then he spoke again to Marshall and pointed at the humans.

Marshall nodded and turned to Mangnas, "Keep in mind all that has been said and now hear the Dar'Wannian plan. It is as follows:

"We will populate this planet with our people at a rate that will allow for an orderly evacuation of your people over the same time frame. The relocation of our population, plants, animals and necessary equipment will take the majority of the next 200 of your years. We will begin with the necessary science, engineering and military to prepare the planet with those elements we will need and then emphasize the young of child-bearing age. Our numbers are substantial and the process of relocating those who could survive the travel and adapt to your different climates and resources might take that full amount of time. We will not be transporting our elderly, sick or any criminals. They will all remain on Dar'Wan along with most of the slave population. The vessels we will use will be provided with enough fuel to reach Earth with our people, transport your people to a new location on another planet within a limited distance and return to Dar'Wan to repeat the process.

"Once a reasonable population is achieved, we will use this planet as a base for further exploration of your galaxy. There are undoubtedly numerous other planetary systems that could benefit us both.

"We will occupy this planet as the prime species. If that would necessitate a military action, we are prepared to do whatever is necessary. You may choose to leave peacefully, or we can force you out. Our objective is to provide for, and protect, our people and this planet is the best means to achieve that end."

Mangnas listened and replied, "The people of this planet will not bow down to such demands. We have a terrible history of battles and wars wherein millions of lives were lost fighting amongst ourselves. Together the nations of Earth will present a formidable front. Attack if you will, but we are not so many sheep to be herded to slaughter. This is our home, and we will defend it."

"Once again," replied Marshall in translation, "I understand your hesitance, but we are the superior species, and we will occupy this planet."

"To that end, we will destroy you if we must. We do not wish a war," continued Flamnar, "that would only destroy the planet and its infrastructure, and result in the deaths of many on both sides. A war is not necessary, and we can assist you in your relocation to another world, one where you will flourish, but we would not. Our taking this planet is the only solution. There will be no further discussion."

"Again," returned Mangnas, "what you are asking is quite impossible."

Flamnar raised his voice and Marshall said calmly, "You misunderstand, I am not asking, I am telling you!" The communication ended abruptly.

Mangnas hurried out to the larger room and addressed the gathered crowd, "Ladies and gentlemen, we have a very serious problem," and he allowed a replay of the conversation with Flamnar. "I suggest the leaders assembled here all return to the safety of the planet's surface and reconvene on our usual network."

The crowd was noticeably angered by the threats issued by Flamnar, but all agreed with Mangnas. The leaders and their teams went to their ships and departures began immediately. Darce approached Kearsay, "General, you should also go to the surface with President Carsteen."

"And what will you do, Captain Gannon?"

"I'll find my commander and get a tach bird," replied Darce.

"As I thought," said Kearsay. "First, I'd like you to pilot our return vehicle, then join Colonel Hansby on the surface."

"Aye, sir," said Darce, "does President Carsteen's transport have a crew?"

"They've already left, taking the secretary general and his team back to the surface."

"I'll find us a bird."

"It may have to be that trash hauler of yours," said Kearsay, "if it can handle passing through the atmosphere."

"You're a very trusting soul, sir," said Darce. "It should be able to handle the re-entry process, but one way or the other, this would be its final trip. We'd need a major league rocket to get it back up here."

An hour later Darce was piloting WSA-C3459 to the surface with Carsteen, Bracken and Jason on board. At the same time, Flamnar was on board the Enkar Tarb, preparing to leave the area near SW-27. He ordered a pass around the Earth to survey the planet's space-based defenses then turn toward the Kuiper Belt and depart the Solar System going back to Da'Wan.

*　　*　　*

EIGHT

2245.11.16.14.36 (Zulu) Transport hub in Northern Virginia

The several rotating space stations around Earth, Moon, Mars and Saturn were all put on high alert. SW-14, named the Hawking, in orbit outside the outer ring around Saturn, was the most distant from Earth. Even though it was fully armed and staffed, all unnecessary occupants were immediately ordered to relocate to the nearest station closer to Earth. The Martian stations, SW-6 and SW-15 began evacuating to the Lunar stations, SW-12 and 18. A full transport from every station to Earth of all superfluous personnel, numbering in the thousands, would take over three years and the entire space station command was left with skeleton operational and tach bird crews. All tach birds were checked, brought up to the highest standard, fully armed and prepared for combat against the unknown power, weaponry and agility of the alien force.

Colonel Hansby needed a dependable pilot to transport herself and senior staff around the planet and to the three Earth-based space stations. Darce and Jason had been initially assigned to the SW-13 defense squadron along with twenty-three other teams. Now they were called back to take President Carsteen back out to SW-27 in a small freighter loaded with basic supplies and ammunition for the station.

"We'll try to slow them down with more conversation," said Hansby. "President Carsteen will invite them to SW-27 to sit down and talk."

"How much time can we expect to gain?" asked Darce.

"No idea," returned Hansby. "We're flying blind on this one. We'll ask and hope they agree to a meeting."

"You think they'll talk?" queried Darce.

"They want this planet with all its systems operable so, yeah, I think they'll talk," she said.

Carsteen entered the room, "Darce, this may be a one-way trip, are you up for that?"

"Aye, sir," replied Darce.

"It'll get us back up there where we can do some good," said Jason as he finished an inspection of the freighter.

"Jason, you don't have to do this," said Darce.

"Yeah, right," returned Jason. "Let you fly up there on your own, you'd probably turn the wrong way in the clouds and be lost for a month. No, you need me."

Carsteen looked impatient and Darce said, "We'll get you back up there, sir but this freighter has no weapons at all. We'll be sitting targets if they decide to fire on us."

"It's not a matter of choice, Captain. Let's get there and worry about them firing on us if that happens."

"Aye, sir," returned both Jason and Darce.

Colonel Bracken arrived with a briefcase full of documents and a duffle bag full of sidearms. "I'll put the duffle in a storage compartment, but we all know where it is if we need it."

They boarded the freighter as Colonel Hansby approached, "Room for one more?"

Carsteen considered before answering, "Best you stay here, keep in touch and be ready to fight from here, Colonel."

She reluctantly stepped back, "Aye sir."

"Colonel," said Carsteen, "no chatter on the com-link, these characters are probably listening to everything we say."

"Understood sir," replied Hansby. "We should maintain normal communications. I'll make a written list of new coded words or phrases. Give me about five minutes."

*   *   *

2245.11.16.17.32 (Zulu) Aboard Freighter

As they began their assent, Carsteen sent a message to Marshall and Flamnar requesting a private meeting aboard SW-27. He hinted that the American nations might be willing to allow the Dar'Wannian suggested process to occur, "I'll buy as much time as I can," he said to Colonel Bracken, "I'll tell them it will take several months to prep an orderly process to begin."

Bracken didn't look happy, "If they suspect you're playing them, it could go very badly."

Carsteen took a deep breath, exhaled and said, "You have a better idea?"

"No sir," Bracken replied, "I wish I did."

They arrived as a squadron of six invader Cains were still holding position, prepared for an attack on SW-27. The attack had been stopped before it began because of Carsteen's message, and the invader Cains were ready to retreat behind the Karnis Tarb.

"Get us on board 27, Darce, then get ready for a punch in the nose," said Carsteen. "I don't trust these bogies."

"Aye sir," came two replies simultaneously.

2245.11.16.21.46 (Zulu) Aboard SW 27

Carsteen assembled the station's senior staff. "I'm going to try to buy us some time by making them an offer, as if I'm willing to discuss an accommodation on the North American continent and I hope they hear me and want to talk about it." He and Bracken went into General Kearsay's office and hailed the Karnis.

* * *

Darce stood in the middle of the bay as Jason stepped off the freighter carrying the duffle bag of weapons. "We need a bird," said Darce "I don't see one. Let's check the other bays, see what's available."

"Slim pickins', Captain," said Tetra as she walked into the bay. "They're all committed to a crew and half of them are on patrol."

"Nothing?" questioned Darce, hopeful she hadn't considered every possibility.

"Well, there is one," said Tetra. "She's an older model, initially launched in '04, but still operable ... I think."

Darce looked at Jason, "Forty-one, and she's still in use?"

"No, gents. Forty-one and still capable," said Tetra. "She was last used to move the larger asteroids out of harm's way several years ago."

Jason looked at Tetra, "No offense Major, but we need something with a serious bite."

Tetra smiled, "I've been working on this bird in my free time for three years. She's old but still has a bite, as you say." She grinned, "How about ten conventional missiles and four larger missiles with little nuclear warheads."

"The type they used to move asteroids?" quizzed Jason.

Tetra smiled again, "Come with me gents, let me introduce you."

They walked to the next maintenance bay and Tetra pulled a tarp off her pet project. "The Blue Wolf, gentlemen. I guess now is as good a time as any to check her out."

"You haven't tried her out yet?" asked Darce.

"No, so let's get her ready to move," returned Tetra.

"There's nothing else," said Darce. "It's this or we sit here and wait to get hit."

Tetra looked at Jason, "Sergeant, you handle the weapons." She turned to Darce, "Captain, I've massaged a lot of the systems on board, but you're still a better pilot than I ever was. You drive, I'll sit second seat."

Darce looked at the logo painted on the side, a blue wolf's head, "Does this beast have a bite?"

Tetra smiled, "Depends on your driving and the sergeant's aim. We can load both missile racks each getting three missiles with conventional warheads and one nuke. That leaves us with four conventional and two more nukes for a second round so, yeah, Captain we have a bite and some sizable teeth."

Jason stepped closer, "And where do you store these little firecrackers?"

Tetra grinned, "This way Sergeant."

* * *

2245.11.16.23.22 (Zulu) Aboard the Blue Wolf

An hour later four missiles, each with a five-kiloton warhead, were unlocked and readied in firing position.

Jason grinned, "These nukes were made for moving asteroids. So, they have variable distance detonation capability. The four already loaded are fives and we have three, two Kt's and three one Kt's. With each of these, the closer they were, the more force they deliver to the target."

"And if one actually hit a target?" quizzed Darce. "What then?"

"In the case of the alien Karnis Tarb type vessels," Jason replied thoughtfully, "I think very serious damage would be delivered within 100 meters, but the closer, the better. Hit the damn thing and it's 'game over.'"

"What about those smaller things, the Tarb Cains?" said Darce.

"I think any cluster of their birds should be a target," returned Jason. "Any detonation within the same 100 meters could seriously damage or destroy the Cains. Again, the closer the better and anyone of them within 2,000 meters of a detonation would most likely feel something." He paused for a moment, "I wonder if they're susceptible to an EMP *(electromagnetic pulse.)*"

"Okay, let's be clear," said Darce, "we don't want to be in the area when one of these babies detonates so, we fire it off and *then* move away?"

"I'd say, enter all target information first, begin to move away," replied Jason, "then loose the little devil and accelerate. When we used these things on asteroids, we defined a target on the asteroid or near it, moved a few kilometers away and let her rip."

"And the EMP?" wondered Darce aloud.

"Naw," replied Jason, "all our circuits are hardened against that." He looked at Tetra, "Major?"

"Right, all systems on board this bird are hardened."

"So, are you two ready to go huntin'?" posed Darce.

"I haven't had a chance to take her out on a test flight," returned Tetra, "so, be careful, Captain."

"Copy that," he returned as the three boarded the Blue Wolf.

A quick review of the controls with Tetra, and Darce was ready to energize the engines. He opened communication with the maintenance bay officer. "Blue Wolf ready to lift off."

"Roger that," returned the officer, "bay doors opening. Good luck Blue Wolf."

The doors opened and Darce energized the lifters raising the ship about a meter off the deck and slowly engaged the forward thrusters. The Blue Wolf responded smoothly as they exited the station's maintenance bay and moved a hundred meters away and stabilized.

* * *

The maintenance bay doors closed, and the Blue Wolf was floating free in space. "Okay Major, let's see what your little toy can do."

Tetra smiled and said, "Ready when you are Captain."

Darce guided the ship forward, then banked left, then right. "Let's take a spin around the station," he said as he pushed the control forward and the old tach bird responded to the series of several simple commands, turning and moving in controlled flight. Tetra looked pleased; her project was working better than she had hoped. "What do you think, Captain?"

"We got us a Bird," said Darce.

Jason glanced at the missile bay, "No Darce. We got us a Wolf."

Darce turned toward his two mates, "Ya know, about 1,200 years ago my family formed the nucleus of an Irish Clann and their symbol was a wolf." Then he smiled and turned his attention to the space in front of them.

Jason buckled in at his station, "I'm gonna check out the targeting system and verify the launch mechanism," he said.

"Maneuverability," said Darce, "let's fly around a bit more and check out the turning and positioning capabilities."

"I'm with you on that," said Tetra.

Jason entered a series of commands into the weapons console, "We have precision targeting capability with these little devils. All I have to do is define the target, tag it and they'll chase it 'til they're within the set targeting distance."

"Then what?" asked Darce.

"Then BOOM!" said Jason, "Like a very large boom and we don't want to be in the neighborhood when it detonates."

* * *

NINE

2245.11.16.23.42 (Zulu) Aboard Station SW-27

Carsteen's communication with Marshall took over two hours, during which, the Earth forces and the SW-27 tach birds began to prepare for an inevitable attack. Carsteen came out of Kearsay's office and walked over to General Kearsay, "I don't think they bought our pitch, General. How many personnel are still on board?"

"Less than a hundred," said Kearsay. "The tach bird crews, basic station operational people and the few of us in this room."

* * *

2246.11.17.03.37 (Off-World) Aboard Karnis Tarb

Flamnar entered the bridge and took Marshall aside, "We now begin attacking the Earth stations, SW-13 and 27. Destroy all their tach birds and take control of both station operations. We will take as many prisoners as we can, so don't kill them all. A large transport vessel had been sent to resupply the Tarbs and their Cains and take any prisoners back to Dar'Fost."

As Flamnar was speaking, a large vessel appeared out of hyperspace just outside the Kuiper Belt and began to navigate through the asteroids. "The Mulbor Kray has arrived," said Marshall.

"Dispatch three Cains immediately," said Flamnar. "They are to protect the Kray and send the remainder of our Cains to attack both of the space stations."

* * *

2245.11.17.05.22 (Zulu) Aboard Station SW-13

The personnel aboard SW-13 located inside the Kuiper belt, noted the aggressive movements of the Cains and signaled an alert to all Earth forces. The station commander responded by sending all twelve of their tach birds out to patrol the immediate area and, if necessary, meet the invaders.

The tach birds were a traditional swept wing configuration with pilot and co-pilot positions side by side and a weapons position behind the co-pilot. The craft was configured with a top mounted docking collar, a pair of missile platforms above and below the wings, twelve directional thrusters and landing gear for ground-based runways. The vehicle was four meters across, three meters high and twelve meters long. The four missile launch platforms were complete with automatic reloading systems with a full magazine of four missiles each. The launch and guidance mechanism allowed the missiles to be launched from any position and either locked in targeting or manual controlled flight. The missile warheads were single blocks of a plastic explosive that could damage a Cain if detonated within 10 meters. A direct or penetrating hit could completely destroy the Cain. Similarly, a direct hit on a Tarb could seriously damage the unit beyond repair or flight in hyperspace.

The Cains were triangular shaped, approximately ten meters on each side and twelve meters across the rear panel. The Cains weaponry consisted of a single energy tube approximately 10 centimeters in diameter protruding from the front point of the craft and two, three-centimeter tubes, one midway on each side. The rear panel had the main engine and four directional thrusters evenly spaced. The Cains had very little ability to maneuver the main energy cannon, only a few centimeters in any direction from a center point. The smaller cannons on the sides had similar restrictions in movement. The limited maneuverability of all three cannons required the Cain to be pointed almost directly at its target before firing an energy burst.

Each burst was measured by the damage it could inflict on its target. Depending on the intensity and location of an energy burst strike, the tach birds would experience differing levels of damage. A full, one-second energy blast with a spread of a two-degrees and a range of less than two kilometers from a Cain's central cannon would obliterate a tach bird. The Cain could only use such a full power burst four times before requiring energy input. Thus, the bursts were kept to a lower level, approximately one-eighth full power, allowing about thirty effective bursts that could seriously damage a tach bird.

The Cain pilots selected their power levels and burst times as the battle progressed. Two Cains chose to use full power and a lengthy burst using all their energy in less than five minutes, Both were blasted by the tach birds as they limped back to their Tarbs for charging of their fuel cells.

The Cains were not as flexible as the tach birds in flight and had difficulty aiming their cannons at a moving target. Six Cains spaced about twenty meters apart, began an attack on the tach birds patrolling outside SW-13. Their initial volley of energy bursts destroyed one tach bird and seriously damaged another.

The other bursts missed their intended targets and streaked into the Kuiper belt striking several asteroids and tossing debris deeper into the belt.

"Station Command, this is TB-06. I've been hit but think I can make it back to a maintenance bay, please advise."

"TB-06, approach the 'C ring', portal 3," returned the Portal Controller, "we'll guide you in."

As TB-06 was being pulled aboard the station, four more tach birds launched, spread out and began searching for Cains. TB-12 locked in on a Cain that was trying to reposition in order to release another burst on another tach bird. "Locked," said TB-12's weapons officer. "Fire when ready Captain."

The two-meter-long missile followed a curved path from the tach bird's platform to the targeted Cain, striking it near one of the mid-point cannons and detonating as it pierced the outer shell. The Cain and crew were scattered in space leaving dangerous debris floating in the nothingness.

Two more tach birds were destroyed by energy bursts and another Cain fell victim to a missile. Neither Cains nor tach birds could maneuver quickly, requiring long turning arcs and very little time to aim weapons. As devastating as the Cains with their energy cannons were, they had difficulty locking onto the tach birds and energy bursts were often wasted into the depths of space. The Borster Tarb moved through several dimensions from hyperspace to normal space outside the Ort Cloud and began navigating through the bits and pieces of rock and ice. They were able to clear both Ort and Kuiper and came to a position less than 1,000 kilometers from SW-8 where they immediately released six Cains, two to stand guard around the Borster and the other four to begin an attack on the rotating space station.

The Enkar Tarb was less than an hour behind the Borster and exited hyperspace closer to SW-13, deployed four Cains to aid in the attack on the station and two others to remain in protective status around the Enkar.

The increase in the number of Cains around the Earth-based space stations gave advantage to the Dar'Wannians and the Earth forces were slowly being defeated in greater numbers than the Dar'Wannians.

* * *

2245.11.17.12.27 (Zulu) Space surrounding SW-13

The Battle continued for hours, and the time as kept on the surface, passed to the next day. The pilots didn't notice the passing of time as they were never in the shadow of the Earth. Tired as they were, the pilots continued the fight as long as they could. The Cains were less maneuverable than the tach birds but had superior firepower, resulting in dogfight scenarios where they were all but equal. The first of the tach birds to be destroyed resulted from an energy burst delivered from a tube mounted on the side of a Cain. The burst was directed at the tach bird and crossed the space between them at light speed. There was no time for the bird to take evasive action. The second it was fired upon, it was hit. There was no targeting lock, no estimating of movement, just sight the target and fire. The tach birds had missiles that had to lock on to a target and needed time to cross the space between them allowing the Cains time to maneuver and possibly avoid a missile strike.

In the initial phases of the battle, the tach bird pilots noticed the speed with which the energy discharges from the Cains crossed space and struck their targets. They adapted by moving in more unpredictable patterns, they began to move erratically to prevent the Cains from aiming at them and avoid the energy bursts.

The fighting was furious and seemed to go in the direction of the Earth based force at several points, but after several hours of energy bursts and missile firings, there was just one tach bird left.

"Station Command, this is TB-1314. I'm down to one missile. Can I re-arm?"

"TB-1314, you're alone out there, fire that last missile and try to reach portal 7," said Station Command.

His last missile locked onto a Cain and pursued it until it was less than a kilometer from the Tarb. The missile caught the Cain as it slowed to approach its docking collar on the Tarb. The explosion destroyed the Cain and severely damaged the Tarb.

TB-1314 turned toward the station and accelerated around the side away from the Tarb. He located Portal 7 and hurried his approach, hooking to the collar clamps and releasing control to the portal controller. He was seconds from opening the hatchway to the maintenance bay when another Cain came around the Station and sent an energy burst that obliterated his tach bird with him still on board.

*　　*　　*

2245.11.17.15.26 (Off-World)　　Space surrounding SW-13

The tach birds had managed to destroy seven of the invading Cains, but the central vessel, the Borster Tarb, similar to the Karnis Tarb, fired its main weapon, blasting a large gap in SW-13's outer ring. A second blast struck the central column, and the station immediately broke into as many smaller sections as possible. Power and life-support systems were damaged. The rotation was slowed to a near stop and the artificial gravity practically canceled. Weightlessness prevented normal functioning of the crew and the station was hit again, breaking a complete quarter of the outer ring away from the center column. As the pieces of the station's outer ring drifted away from the center column, some moved into the Kuiper belt where they would most likely be destroyed.

The surviving complement of approximately two-thousand personnel were captured and immediately transferred aboard a large transport vehicle, the Mulbor Kray. They were destined for a planet in the Perdone Galaxy, Dar'Fost.

The Mulbar Kray was a large vessel meant to move troops, and hardware into combat zones and was also well suited for moving prisoners. The vessel was large, cylindrical shaped over two hundred meters in length and thirty meters in diameter. As it approached near the Station, a gravitational field was established, and a shield formed around the Station allowing the Dar'Wannian soldiers to herd prisoners into the transport's cargo bay. Prisoners were being sorted by degree of injury and apparent rank. Prisoners were being asked who was in charge of the survivors and nine higher ranking officers were gathered in a room aboard the transport.

"My name is Kayla Trann, I am the commander of this transport vessel, the Mulbor Kray. You will tell your people we are taking you to an Earth like planet, Dar'Fost, where you will be resettled.

We do not execute or confine prisoners in cages, we resettle them out of our way.

*　　*　　*

2245.11.17.18.17 (Zulu)　　Space surrounding SW-27

The Tarb Cains from Karnis deployed into an attack formation and the strike on SW-27 began. All 12 tach birds aboard SW-27 were deployed. The initial encounters were like boxers dancing around the ring, looking for weak spots. Then the fighting became intense, and the tach birds were destroyed at twice the number of Cains. Darce, Tetra and Jason readied their Blue Wolf and moved to the active battle area. A cluster of six remaining Cains came at them from behind the Karnis. Tetra sited the cluster, Jason entered a few commands and called to Darce, "Ready on nuke one."

Darce turned the ship, fired the nuke and accelerated away. The missile was perceived as an impact weapon and the Dar'Wannians were about to allow it to pass through the center of their group. When it reached the middle of the cluster, it detonated. The blast destroyed four of the Cains and rocked the Karnis. Immediately the remaining two Cains sped toward the Blue Wolf. Too close to use another nuke and with no other weapons available, Darce tried to maneuver the Blue Wolf away from the rotating station. The Cains both discharged weapons, hitting the Blue Wolf's left side near the primary engine. Tetra said, "We're far enough away from the Karnis, let's unload on it and hope for the best."

Darce responded, "Jason, you got 'em targeted?" "Aye Cap," shouted Jason, "let's give 'em hell."

Darce fired the remaining three nukes at the Karnis and pulled away. The Karnis responded immediately, firing a blast from their underside hitting the nukes less than a kilometer from their ship. The detonation knocked one of the Cains into an uncontrollable spin toward the Earth's surface. The Karnis was damaged. The remaining Cain attacked the Blue Wolf, inflicting serious damage and limiting its ability to maneuver. Darce managed to slowly guide the Blue Wolf back into the maintenance bay and after the doors closed, Tetra began inspecting the damage.

"We might be able to get her out there again," said Tetra, "but without missiles."

"So, we're out of options," said Carsteen. "All our tach birds are damaged or destroyed and this station has no defensive weapons. Our engineers are trying to modify the guns from the damaged tach birds, but that may take hours and there are no guarantees."

"Sir," said a maintenance bay operator, "they're demanding that we open the bay doors and let the Cain enter."

“Or?” quizzed Carsteen.

“Or—they’ll destroy the station.”

Carsteen looked at Darce and Jason, “Find Kearsay. Do we still have evacuation capability? If so, when can we begin?”

Tetra found Kearsay, he was in the large conference room with a group of about eighty people. “Sir, the president is in the maintenance bay. He’s asking if we have any remaining evacuation capability.”

Kearsay looked at a technician, “How many pods are left, and can we get all these people in them?” He turned toward Tetra, “Is your tach bird operable?”

“No sir, we limped aboard,” said Tetra. “We’d never make it to the surface.”

“I’m not thinking of going to the surface,” said Kearsay. “I’m debating between a surrender and flying your bird into the Karnis.”

“Darce could probably control the Blue Wolf well enough to get to the Karnis.”

“No,” said Kearsay, “You three must get to the surface. Our pilots need to know how the Cains fight. We’re being told to surrender SW-27, or they will destroy the station and kill us all.”

“Sir, have you ever flown one of these birds?” asked Tetra as she pointed toward the maintenance bay.

“I don’t have to pilot the damn thing, just point it at the Karnis and let her rip.”

Darce approached, put a hand on Kearsay’s shoulder, “Sir, that’s my job, you belong here or on the surface with the people.”

As he was speaking, Carsteen and Bracken entered the room. “What’s the status?” asked Carsteen.

The technician returned and said, "We can get most of the people in the pods, but not all. Some of us are going to have to stay on board."

"Get me a link to the Karnis," said Carsteen, "now!"

Two minutes later in the General's office, Carsteen opened a channel to the Karnis, "To whom do I speak?"

"I am Koston Hylak, Commander of the Karnis Tarb. Who are you?"

"I am Jacob Carsteen."

"Ah, Mr. President, do you surrender Station number 27?"

"On the condition that we be allowed to evacuate the station in our escape pods," returned Carsteen.

"Please understand, Mr. President, you are one of our objectives," said Hylak. "If you are not captured, we might as well destroy the station with all on board."

Carsteen looked at Kearsay, "Okay, I'm going to surrender to the aliens, and you have the station with the remaining personnel."

"We can't fully evacuate the station," said Kearsay, "there'll be thirty-eight of us still on board after the deployment."

Carsteen looked at Bracken, "I want you on the surface, Colonel." He then turned to Tetra, "You as well, Major."

"I will leave when General Kearsay leaves, sir," returned Harmon.

Darce was about to interject when Carsteen said, "Major, it has been my pleasure and honor to have worked with you."

Harmon smiled, tilted her head to one side then turned and walked back into the General's office. Darce was again about to speak when Carsteen said, "Kearsay told me, she's an amazing soldier. Brilliant, a bit hard-headed, and impossible to argue with when she sets her mind." He looked at Darce, "Shall we?"

"Aye, sir."

The Karnis was again contacted, "We are ready to deploy our pods."

Hylak hesitated then, "Yes, our sensors so indicate. They will be allowed to reach the surface, then you will be taken prisoner and brought here. If there is any deception, the pods will be tracked and destroyed as well as the station."

"Darce, are we ready to move out?" asked Carsteen.

"Aye sir, as ever was," returned Darce.

Hylak hailed the station, "You may release the pods. I trust all is as we discussed?"

"It is," said Carsteen, "and there are about 38 people still aboard this Station."

"As long as you abide by the agreement, none of your people will be harmed. Do we understand each other?"

Carsteen replied, "I do."

* * *

2245.11.17.22.06 (Zulu) Space surrounding SW-27

The pods were released, and each was tracked by the Dar'Wannians. As the last one reached the upper atmosphere and began to heat up, Carsteen opened the channel to Hylak, "I am ready to come aboard the Karnis, but our remaining tach bird is seriously damaged. It will take a while to approach."

"You may begin," returned Hylak, "we'll assist you as needed."

Carsteen struggled at the controls and Darce said, "Not to worry sir, we'll get you there."

"Darce, I appreciate all you've done for me, but they probably won't let you leave once I'm delivered. Show me how to drive this crazy thing and I'll either make it there or crash it into the Karnis."

Jason looked at Darce, "You think they'll keep us both?" he asked with a grin. "Bastards don't know what they've bargained for."

Carsteen said, "You two stay here, I'll handle this myself."

Jason looked at the president, "Ain't no way I'm gonna sit on my ass while you run around out there and get yourself killed. If they're lookin for a fight, I'll give 'em one to remember."

Darce looked at Carsteen, "There's your answer, Mr. President."

* * *

TEN

2245.11.17.22.36 (Zulu) Aboard the Blue Wolf

Darce took the pilot's seat and began the start sequence. The primary engine would not energize. Jason opened the hatch, stepped out to check the engine when Tetra yelled out, "Cut the power, you burned out one coil and you're over stressing the last two."

"Burned out?" said Jason, "Are we dead in the water here?"

Tetra ran to her work bench, grabbed a bag of tools, and said, "Climb aboard, you can help me." She pulled the hatch closed, opened an internal panel near the primary engine, and began working deep inside the panel. Five minutes later she said, "Tell Darce to bring the secondary engine, number two, up slowly. Then when I signal, he can start the primary engine."

"We got this, Major," said Jason, "you can get off now."

Tetra looked at Jason, "Sergeant, man the navigation station. You may have to depend on visuals."

Darce started the secondary engine and brought the power up. Tetra moved into the co-pilot seat and said, "You can start the primary engine now—slowly Captain."

The craft shuddered as the primary engine came to life. Darce looked at Tetra and smiled, "Say when."

Tetra checked the control panel displays and nodded, "When you're ready, Captain."

The Blue Wolf rumbled to a higher level of life and Darce began the lift off. "Open outer doors and standby for weightlessness."

Tetra, Carsteen and Jason checked their restraints as the Wolf moved outside the station and Darce slowly accelerated to a reasonable cruising speed.

*   *   *

2245.11.17.24.28 (Off-World)   Aboard the Karnis Tarb

The trip to the Karnis was bumpy. Tetra and Jason were very busy adjusting, crossing wires and praying. The Blue Wolf finally came to rest outside the Karnis' landing area and Darce waited for an indication to proceed. As the doors to the landing area opened, he inched the Blue Wolf forward. As he set it down on the deck, another panel popped, sizzled and sparked. Jason looked at Tetra, "Think we can get a cab home, 'cause this buggy ain't goin' anywhere." The doors to the Karnis' exterior closed, the area pressurized, and a gravitational field was energized.

A cadre of soldiers stood at the door as Carsteen, Tetra, Jason and Darce exited the Blue Wolf. A Dar'Wannian in a red tunic with eight chevrons on his sleeve approached, "I am Koston Hylak. He looked at all four. His eyes rested on Carsteen, "Mr. President, please come this way."

Carsteen hesitated, "Can these people be taken back to SW-27?"

Hylak responded immediately, "No, Major Harmon, Captain Gannon and Sergeant Leary will not be released."

Jason tilted his head, raised an eyebrow, and said, "They're asking us to stay, how nice."

"Allow me to inform the staff on the station that we have arrived and will be staying," said Carsteen.

Hylak nodded in approval as Carsteen tapped his communicator, "Colonel Stanley, we are on board the Karnis Tarb and will be staying. Please inform Colonel Bracken to notify the Vice President that he is now in charge."

"Will do sir," returned Stanley. "Any further instructions?"

"No, that will be all, Colonel," returned the president.

The captured Earthlings were escorted into another room where several Dar'Wannians were waiting for them, "We will be going back to Dar'Wan," said Marshall. "Our military will have many questions for all four of you." He paused thoughtfully, motioned to Hylak and in their language said, *"We want them comfortable and ready to discuss their capabilities. They're not going anywhere so, whatever they learn from us would be irrelevant, but anything we learn from them could be useful in our conquest of their planet."*

Hylak agreed and approached Darce, "Captain Gannon, would you like to see this vessel navigate the space between here and Dar'Wan?"

Darce looked at Jason and Tetra, "We'd all like to see that," he said with a nod.

"Yes sir," added Jason, "see how your ship stacks up against ours."

Carsteen raised his hand, "Excuse me, what are you doing?"

Tetra looked at the President, winked, and said, "Just gonna look out the window."

Carsteen looked unhappy but understood. *These three are already planning our escape.*

* * *

Koston Hylak was very proud of his Karnis Tarb, "This vessel could accommodate forty people for a journey such as this. The trip will take approximately seven of your days to get us to Dar'Wan."

"Dar'Wan is over twenty-lightyears from Earth, so you'd be moving at some impossible speed," said Jason as he paused and calculated in his head, "around LS 3. That's amazing."

"We have learned to use different forms of energy," returned Hylak. "Our vessels were restricted to travel within our own galaxy and with the impending collision, some of this arm of your Milky Way. Our developments with this energy led us to new potentials almost every day and thus we've been able to search many new worlds looking for our new home over the last hundred of our years."

"What do you mean by different forms of energy?" asked Jason.

Hylak felt the hook going in deeper, "That's something which you would call classified. It's a secret, and I'm not permitted to talk about it even to my own people."

Jason knew when to back off and turned his questions to the controls of the ship at these higher speeds. "My god, if you hit anything, even something very small, it could tear this vessel apart."

"Very true, Sergeant, there is an energy shield surrounding this vessel. Actually, the energy bubble extends into our intended path. The gravitational anchors both attract and repel so any smaller bits of material are pushed aside, the larger are avoided. We use our weapons to break up larger things and then push them out of the way. Now, if you don't mind, I should be on the bridge." He looked at Darce, "You may come with me."

Standing on the bridge, Darce, Tetra and Jason all noticed their bodies feeling heavier. Hylak noted the change as well and commented, "We are adjusting the atmospheric conditions on board to those we will experience on Dar'Wan. You will notice the air has a slightly different taste and smell. The oxygen content is increased, and the nitrogen is decreased. The crew, as well as yourselves, need an adjustment period during this trip."

There were seven Dar'Wanian personnel on the bridge, each at a control panel with several view screens and a padded surface slightly taller and wider than the individual directly behind them. Koston Hylak went to a central station, leaned back against his pad, and touched his view screens one at a time. "Captain Gannon, you may appreciate this. Come see."

Darce approached Hylak cautiously, "Appreciate?"

"It will be easier to see on the main view screen," said Hylak as he brought a large screen, 10 meters wide and 5 meters high, to life in front of the assembled crew. "This is a view directly in front of us. See there in the center of the screen, that spot of light. That star is our first objective in this trip. We have named it 'Consor'. It means 'the final turn'. As we leave our planet and venture out in the direction of your planet, it is the last star we use in making a turn and the first star or turn on our way home."

"How many turns are made in a journey to Earth?" asked Darce.

"In all, there will be five such adjustments before we reach Dar'Wan," returned Hylak.

Darce looked at the small spot of light and noticed other spots turn to streaks and disappear off both sides of the view screen, "The final turn? So named while coming to Earth from Dar'Wan. Amazing, how fast are we going?"

"In your terms, we have passed the LS 0 and LS 1 levels. We will achieve somewhere in the LS 4 level when we stabilize in the next leg of our journey," replied Hylak.

Jason and Tetra were walking between the several crew members, trying to understand what they were doing at their stations. "You say LS 4?" Jason asked, looking at Hylak, "That would be impossible with the propulsion engines we use."

"True enough," said Darce, "just how do you power these vessels?"

"Hylak smiled, "Aah, our secrets, if your people had this technology years ago as we did, things might have been very different." He hesitated and continued, "The Talmonoria are probably close to revealing it to you anyway."

As they were talking, Marshall and Carsteen entered the bridge, "Kolston, we've come to see the stars," said Marshall.

"We were just discussing the energy source for this vessel," returned Hylak.

"Of course," said Marshall, "you must be very curious. Please continue, Kolston."

"So, you were saying?" said Jason.

"So," continued Hylak, "the energy we use to power these vessels, as well as our systems on Dar'Wan, is partially due to what you refer to as Dark Energy."

"Dark energy," began Darce, "how?"

"Admittedly, we had help," said Hylak. "A number of years ago, long before my time, the Talmonoria determined we would benefit with a more complete knowledge of this Dark Energy. We were on the verge of understanding several previously unknown dimensions and they provided clues to discovering the pieces of the puzzle allowing us to capture and use dark energy to travel through hyperspace."

"I'm sure the impending destruction of our planet was the reason they shared this technology," said Marshall.

"They didn't tell us everything," said Hylak. "Just enough for us to develop limited power systems for space travel and everyday consumption on Dar'Wan."

Marshall added, "We have a long way to go, but we've been able to travel about our galaxy and explore parts of yours. We had established several remote stations to refuel and restock vital supplies, however, our current level of development has all but eliminated that need. The stations are now mostly abandoned, still functional, but unused. The biggest problem is the collection, storage and control of this form of energy. It took a long time to collect enough energy to allow us to come to earth in this one vessel without stopping at the stations."

Carsteen asked, "How do you collect energy?"

"I have no way of knowing," replied Marshall. "The engineers and scientists have constructed several very large collection centers over the last 100 of our years, the most recent to replace two older installations that are not very productive."

"And how do you store energy?" asked Darce.

Hylak answered, "As Marshall said, we have no way of knowing. The experts handle all of that."

Jason, still watching the crew at their stations asked, "How is it that we can stand as the Karnis accelerates?"

"We manipulate the gravitational forces in and around the vessel," said Hylak.

"All using Dark Energy?" asked Tetra.

"Yes, in ways I don't understand," said Marshall. "Again, our scientists handle all of that," added Hylak.

As the voyage continued, the questions rose and fell, and the Earth team learned more and more of the control of the vessel.

"Captain Gannon," said Hulak, "we will soon experience a course adjustment as we pass the Consor. This requires a very careful observation of the sensors and confirmation of our new bearing before we accelerate to a higher speed for the longest part of this trip."

"How many times will you be making course corrections?" asked Darce.

"Four more as we approach Dar'Wan," said Hylak. Each will require a reduction in speed and end with our insertion in an orbital position above the planet."

* * *

ELEVEN

2245.11.21.16.32 (Off-World) Aboard the Karnis Tarb

As the Karnis established an orbit around Dar'Wan, Hylak brought up a view of the planet's surface for the four aliens to see. "Our home," said Hylak, "we welcome you to Dar'Wan."

The planet resembled Earth in several ways, there were large areas of dark blue, others of rich green, and still others a light brown. The orb was surrounded by a scattering of grey and white clouds.

Hylak gestured toward the view screen, we are establishing orbit at an altitude of 880 kilometers. We will circle the planet several times before we descend to the planet's surface." He paused and again pointed at a brown and green area on the screen, "That land mass is called Wan'Santro, it is approximately the size of your Australia."

As the Karnis continued to orbit, Hylak pointed again, "That is Wan'Tarka, an area about five times that of Santro. You will see other land areas in various sizes and shapes. We will be landing on Wan'Markan, our capital, and center of our scientific community." Hylak then entered a few commands in his console and the view on the main screen changed to one of space. The view moved, scanning the sky and settled on a large orb above the Dar'Wannian horizon. "That is Dar'Fost, another planet in our system. It is quite close to us, only forty-five million kilometers, and remains at that distance as we both circle our star." He noted the interest of the Earthlings and added, "The conditions on Fost are similar to your Earth. Unfortunately, the planet's magnetic field has been degenerating for a very long time and would soon make the planet uninhabitable if it weren't going to be destroyed. We use it as a storage area and prison."

"Is that where we will be taken?" asked Tetra, "To a prison."

"I don't know what the leaders have planned for you," replied Hylak, "initially you are to be delivered to Dar'Wan."

The time-lapse shown on board the Karnis' instrumentation indicated a three-day voyage. Hylak commented to Carsteen, "We have been in route here for six days, but the time-lapse on this planet's surface is closer to seven days.

Marshal entered the room, "I must advise you; this world differs from yours in several ways. As you already know, Dar'Wan is larger and more massive than the Earth and the gravity is thus greater. You may feel extremely tired and weaker here. The composition of the air here also differs. Our oxygen content is greater and the nitrogen a little less. You will feel higher atmospheric pressure, a higher temperature, and the various odors may take some getting used to." He looked about for a reaction and continued, "I hope the few days aboard the Karnis have prepared you for this."

The view screen returned to Dar'Wan and zoomed in to a closer view. The features clearly visible included the deep dark blue oceans, the rich green forests, deserts, mountains, and vast open plains. It looked in many ways, similar to Earth.

"A closer look," Hylak calmly ordered a crew member and the view screen changed to a closer view of a wide area with several smaller rectangular grids and what appeared to be connecting roads. This is our main city; it consists of six centers connected with transport systems and highways. Each center has a business section, a production section, and a living section. If any one of these centers falls, the other five will continue and the sixth will be reconstructed. Each of these centers can sustain itself with as many as three of the others in reconstruction."

Marshall noticed the puzzled look on the faces of the aliens. "Our planet has a very active core with nine major tectonic plates and a few minor ones. The frequency with which we experience a disturbance as one or more of the plates move demands that we spread our people and resources. Buildings are limited in height due to these quakes and the gravitational forces at play here."

"Our buildings are more pyramidal than rectangular in construction," added Hylak. "The frequent shaking of the surface plates would bring down most buildings as you have built them on Earth. Here we begin with a stable base and keep the overall height to a minimum. If one sector suffers damage, we can easily rebuild. Buildings are thus standardized in components and constructed far enough apart to prevent collateral damage from the collapse of one."

"Our world is different," said Carsteen, "we build up as high as we can and very close together. The earthquakes that we suffer do occur, but apparently not with the same frequency as here. Perhaps you would prefer a planet with lower structures."

"The height to which you can build on Earth makes your planet all the more desirable," said Hylak. "We could grow in numbers much more than here on Dar'Wan."

Marshall tapped his communicator several times, "We are now ready to descend to the surface. Please come with me." He led them to the bay where the Blue Wolf had landed. "You call this the Blue Wolf?" he asked.

"Yes," returned Tetra. "It's an older model tach bird, but it flies, or did until one of your Cains hit us near the main engine."

"Well, we may repair it," said Marshall, "If it could prove useful in the future." He led them to his Shom, "We'll use this shuttle to get to the planet's surface."

*   *   *

2245.11.21. (Off-World)   Boarding a Shom on the Karnis Tarb

On board, everyone, including Marshall was stood against tilted padded surfaces and strapped in. The door was closed, and Marshall said, "The descent will take about two of your hours. We will pass through an area where the winds are rather strong, but this craft has made the journey many times." A crew member checked all the securing straps and spoke to Marshall in a strange language then went through a door.

Marshall noticed the looks on the Earthling's faces, "Our pilot, just making sure all is ready for the descent. If you look through the windows, you may see the surface at first, until the pilot aligns the shom. Then, you'll see stars as you have seen from your SW-27 and you may see our main star, similar to your sun. Here it is called Korta, a word loosely translated to 'sky fire.'"

Almost immediately the Shom moved, lifting off the deck and rotating. Darce could see the large outer doors open as the pilot positioned the craft to exit the landing bay. The planet's surface was visible for a moment as the Shom rotated into a flight position and suddenly surged forward. As the Shom passed through the door to space, the feeling of weightlessness occurred and as

Marshall said, the initial view was of stars in the distance, some of which clustered into a long string like the arm of a spiral galaxy.

Marshall noted Darce's observation, "The line of stars you see is what you call the Perdone Galaxy, our galaxy. Now, if you look out the other side, most of the stars you'd see are from your Milky Way."

Jason looked out the opposite side and said, "Where is our system?"

"Probably one of those little dots of light, but I couldn't tell you which one."

The Shom accelerated and began to descend, eventually passing through a layer of heavy clouds and high winds. "This is quite common in our descents and when we return to our space stations," said Marshall. "We should be through it shortly."

As the Shom approached the surface, the feeling of weight returned, the temperature and humidity increased and the air within the Shom took on a different taste and pressure. The landing was gentle, and the pilot returned. He again spoke in a strange language to Marshall and began to loosen the restraints.

Exiting the Shom proved Marshall's description, the air was warmer and the humidity higher, breathing was invigorating, but at the same time, the gravity and temperature were exhausting. The sky was a dark blue and grey clouds raced across the horizon.

"This is the business center of our main city," said Marshall, "we will be meeting with a number of physicians, scientists and others, all with questions and a desire to engage in conversation." He looked at the sky and said, "A storm approaches, we should get inside."

* * *

2245.11.21.XX.XX (Off-World) On Planet Dar'Wan

The four aliens from Earth were taken to a holding area, a 10-meter square room with light grey stone walls, floor, and ceiling. Light entered the space via a 20-centimeter-high slot at the ceiling level around the perimeter, three meters above the floor. There was no furniture or decorations.

"Is this a prison?" questioned Jason.

As he asked, the door opened and Marshall entered, "You are now to be taken to other accommodations which resemble your Earth-bound abodes." He paused as another Dar'Wannian joined him, "This is Garnat Soute, he will take you and be your guide for as long as required. Please understand, we will not be locking you in a cell or restricting your movements about the city. There is no place for you to escape to, nor is there anyone who would assist you in an escape. We want you to become more aware of our civilization, and, after a while, you may see the value in a cooperative effort to accommodate both of our peoples."

"We're free to wander about?" puzzled Jason.

"Yes," replied Garnat, "first there will be meetings which may last days, then I'd be happy to lead you about, show you almost anything you'd like to see."

"Almost?" asked Darce.

"Yes, Captain Gannon, you understand there are some things that are to remain secret, even from our own citizens."

"Understood, but we would really like to know more about Dark Energy."

"I will ask my superiors just what the limits are," said Garnat, "but first, it is my task to find food you determine to be palatable. We have a number of fruits, vegetables, and several types of meat. I have arranged a buffet of a wide assortment for you to sample."

"You don't happen to have any Kentucky Bourbon or a good German beer?" asked Jason.

"I am aware of the wide variety of alcoholic beverages you people consume on Earth. We do not do so here. Our main drinks are water and juices of various fruits." He provided several drinks for the three to sample, "These vegetables are similar to your potato, carrot and beet. I thought we should start here and bring in others as you wish."

The sampling of foods and drinks continued for an hour and the four Earthlings were tired and needed rest. "We can continue this tomorrow if you like, after a meeting with our medical staff."

Each day, the four Earthlings were engaged in meetings with various Dar'Wannians. Each prodding for information about medicine, religion, politics, business, science and military. "They heard us talking about the SSSRD," said Jason with a wry smile.

Darce slowly scanned the room as he replied, "You can't tell anybody about that."

Tetra initially looked puzzled then, as she caught on to the ruse, "Weapons in development or actually being deployed should not be discussed at all."

Carsteen added, "Even I know nothing about it other than it's in development. The less we know, the better."

Jason looked at Darce, "I thought it had gone through some testing, but I agree, the less said, the better."

Darce nodded, and he changed the subject, "Time, we should agree on a time and coordinate with other humans here."

"We did a chronometer check in August on board the Blue Wolf and synced with SW-27. Do you think the travel at the elevated LS level will have affected our instruments?"

I don't know," answered Jason as he checked his wrist device. "I make it 2245.11.21.16.39."

"We appear to be in agreement, so let's stick to our planet's time," said Carsteen.

*　　*　　*

TWELVE

2246.02.25.13.17 (Off-World)   On Planet Dar'Wan

Three months passed on Earth and four large Dar'Wannian vessels assumed positions around the Earth's moon. On Dar'Wan, Carsteen, Darce and Jason had been quizzed, poked and prodded for as much information as the Dar'Wannians could get. The exact nature of the SSSRD was not determined and remained the only apparent reason to continue interrogations. Outside of the SSSRD, the Dar'Wannians tried to demonstrate human like qualities in hopes of using these three as catalysts in occupying the Earth. In that vein, the Earthlings were given near free rein to roam the city and ask questions.

"We have a tour of the city planned to familiarize you with our home," said Garnat. "Now, not all of our citizens speak your language, but some have begun to learn. I will accompany you and translate as needed."

Tetra and Jason showed an interest in machines of all types, and the Dar'Wannians tried to use that interest to their advantage. They toyed with the most basic devices, carefully observing the energy needed to perform even the simplest task.

Eventually, the Blue Wolf was brought down to the planet's surface and Tetra, with Jason and Darce's help, was allowed to check systems and make repairs. The old tach bird was well suited for flight in space as well as Earth's atmosphere, but the gravitational forces existent on Dar'Wan could prevent the Blue Wolf from achieving lift-off, much less reach orbit.

The extreme gravity on Dar'Wan and the thicker, heavier and more humid air made every exercise exhausting. The three Earthlings needed frequent and longer periods of rest during the day. The longer days, the composition of the air, temperature and humidity all different from what they were accustomed to also added to their fatigue.

* * *

Flamnar called Marshall to a closed meeting where the status of the Earthlings was a point of discussion. "Are these four humans worth keeping?" he asked.

"I believe they are," returned Marshall. "We still have not determined the nature of the SSSRD. We are trying to acclimate them to conditions here, we're not having the success we had hoped for."

"Perhaps one of our space-based stations," Flamnar speculated. "We are getting some of our people accustomed to Earth-type conditions. Why not put them there and give them something to do?"

"Yes," said Marshall, "or send them to Dar'Fost, either way, they could occupy themselves repairing their vessel, that Blue Wolf."

Flamnar thought for a moment and said, "Yes, Dar'Fost, make it happen. We should pay close attention and learn all we can about their warship and its weapons."

Garnat approached the four as they were resting after a brief walk about and said, "We will be going up to our Station 16 and take a transport to Dar'Fost. It has conditions which are the closest to your planet. There you will have the same freedom as you have here on this planet's surface."

Tetra said, "I'd really like to stay here and continue working on our tach bird."

"I'll see about having your Blue Wolf sent as well," said Garnat.

Two technicians accompanied the Blue Wolf as it was brought aboard Station 16 and loaded on the transport vessel. "We have configured two power-conversion devices which will allow operation of your systems and tools," said Mabosh, one of the technicians.

The second technician, Kalyx added, "These cylinders are charged energy sources," as he handed Darce a small cylindrical container. "One of these energy sources should provide all the power your Blue Wolf requires for full operation." He handed a second cylinder to Tetra, "The energy source is to be placed in one of these conversion devices," he continued as he placed Darce's cylinder in a small black box with two wires coming out the end of the unit. He pressed a little panel on the box and the panel lit up. "When the panel shows light," he said, "there is power available in these wires. It holds more than your batteries, so you should connect it to your inverter inlet to achieve your desired three-phase power. This one cylinder can provide power to all your systems and allow you to operate your Blue Wolf and recharge your tools."

Tetra looked at the cylinder in her hand, "How do we recharge this?"

Kalyx said, "Do not concern yourself with that, these two energy units will last longer than your vessel." Mabosh placed the second cylinder into another conversion unit and asked where the connection point to the power supply in the ship is located.

Tetra opened a power panel, "The main batteries are connected through a set of contacts behind this plate." She used a screwdriver to remove the plate covering and pointed to three connection lugs. "These three cables are from the main battery and inverter housing. The best place to make the connection would probably be there, in the battery compartment."

Mabosh said, "Your batteries may be recharged or removed, and this conversion unit installed. Which way would you prefer?"

Tetra looked a little confused, thought for a moment, and said, "I'd charge the batteries as much as this little conversion unit can handle."

Mabosh nodded and almost smiled, "This conversion unit and the energy pack should be able to provide power much longer than your batteries. This is a small test of our technology working with your equipment and we are very confident it will work well."

"Could it power our ship on a trip to Earth?" asked Tetra, "Like your Karnis Tarb?"

"The Karnis Tarb was designed and built for such travel, this Blue Wolf is not, but it could power your ship as you have used it in the past."

Jason and Tetra tried to learn more about the Karnis Tarb and its systems that allowed travel at multiples of light speed. "So, could this energy pack power the Karnis for a trip to Earth?"

"No, such a journey would require a much larger power pack," replied Mabosh, "one that I could not easily lift and carry. The process of charging the large packs takes a long time, but the charge in one of them is enough to propel a Karnis type vessel to your planet and back. Perhaps it is similar to your SSSRD."

Darce ignored Mabosh's last statement and asked, "How big are these power packs?"

"You will see soon," said Mabosh, "Our main power collection and storage facility is there."

Jason looked at Darce and Tetra with a sly grin and winked.

* * *

Mabosh was obviously more than a technician. He was looking for information about the weapons and systems which would be used in the defense of Earth. The SSSRD was an unknown and they assumed very secret. Their latest probe did not find any information on that or other possible systems they might encounter. He reported back to Marshall and Flamnar, "I don't know what the SSSRD is or what it can do, but these humans have developed laser and nuclear weapons as a major component of their overall weapons systems. I assume it's probably in the same vein, a weapon of mass destruction."

"That does not fit with our plan," said Flamnar. "We want the planet intact as much as possible. Their nuclear weapons would make huge portions of the planet uninhabitable and that defeats our purpose."

"We know they will not leave peacefully, and military action is apparently not an option," said Marshall, "where does that leave us?"

"There are about ten billion people on planet Earth. We'd have to determine which ones should be moved or eliminated first," began Marshall.

"We could not transport everybody," said Mabosh, "a relocation process of that extent would take years and only those capable of making a long journey would logically be sent."

"You have another solution, Mabosh?" asked Flamnar.

"Considering the time it would take to relocate the people capable of making a trip, the number of vessels we would need to relocate them and the power we would have to collect and dedicate to the relocation, we have a situation that doesn't work."

"Please continue, Mabosh," said Flamnar.

"We will need those vessels and energy to move our own people," said Mabosh. "I would rather we eliminate as many humans as we bring in our people—one for one."

"So, we bring in 100 of our people and kill 100 of the Earthlings?" asked Marshall.

"Yes, perhaps we select the young ones first and allow the older ones to die naturally," said Flamnar, "but the Talmonoria would not like us killing off an entire species they had spent time nurturing."

Mabosh offered, "Yes, and I would not enjoy condemning humans. It would be better if the humans naturally died off."

"Yes," returned Marshall, "but they keep multiplying and their numbers will continue to increase as they have for centuries."

"We could prevent new births," said Mabosh, "sterilize the population and as they continue to naturally die, their population will decrease. Their lifespan is between 100 and 150 of their years so, within that time frame, they would all be gone."

"Our span is over 200 of their years so, we might well see the last of them before the three of us have reached our ending."

"How do we sterilize the entire population of the planet?" asked Flamnar.

"We introduce a virus that would prevent pregnancies," said Mabosh.

"Distribution?" puzzled Flamnar.

Mabosh said, "The water supplies around the planet."

"Do we have such a substance that would sterilize everybody on the planet?" asked Flamnar.

"Not yet," returned Mabosh.

The three Dar'Wannians continued the discussion through the remainder of the day.

*   *   *

THIRTEEN

2246.02.28.09.22 (Off-World) On Planet Dar'Wan

Flamnar called a meeting with the medical and biological experts. As he explained the solution, questions were raised about human test subjects, the development time, and the process of distribution. "Will we be able to get all the people?" asked Marshall.

"We only need to infect the males and females capable of reproduction," said Mabosh. "If we miss small pockets of the people, they may be addressed in other ways."

"So, older humans who are beyond reproduction capability will not be a problem," said Marshall. "I would estimate if we infect a significant portion of the population each year, we could achieve our goal in the same time it will require us to relocate there. As humans die off, we move in peacefully and never disclose our methods."

"Keep in mind, the Talmonoria would not approve of slaughtering an entire civilization," said Flamnar.

"I suggest we identify available test subjects among the prisoners taken in the capture of their Space Station SW-13," said Marshall, "I believe there are about 2,000 prisoners being held on Dar'Fost, a sufficient number should be suitable for testing."

"Agreed," said Flamnar, "how long will the development and testing take?"

Mabosh thought for a moment, "I would guess less than a complete revolution about Korta. However, we're not concerned with side effects so we can rush it through as soon as we have minor success."

"If we introduce a virus that prevents the reproduction of humans, the race will die out in less than 160 of their years. Our timetable would work well with that sequence. As they die out, we introduce more of our population. Within the first sixty years, we would be the predominant species. Another fifty to sixty years and they'll be all but gone."

"So, we wouldn't have to transport them to another planet," said Marshall.

"No," said Mabosh, "and as the population ages, they will become less problematic, maybe even resigned to their roles as slaves."

"We wouldn't need to replace the vessels they would have used," said Flamnar, "and the energy we save could be used for our own people and not wasted on the humans."

Mabosh offered, "Another feature, disposing of the dead humans, we allow them to conduct their normal funerals and cremations."

"Mabosh, you take control of the research and production of the infecting agent," said Flamnar. "Keep it very quiet, even if we have to confine the research team. No word of this can reach any human and that means the four here in this city."

* * *

2246.03.01.14.25 (Off-World) On Planet Dar'Wan

Kalyx took the four Earthlings to a landing pad and ushered them aboard another shuttle. "This Shom will deliver you to Station 16," he said. "There you will be placed aboard a transport vessel and taken to Dar'Fost." He excused himself and went forward to speak to the pilot.

The Earthlings were secured in tilted pads and the Shom's systems were energized. Darce looked at Carsteen, "Have you learned anything new?"

Carsteen responded, "I don't know, it seems all of a sudden the questions about earth's defenses have stopped, it's as if they have their answers—as if they know all they need to know about the SSSRD."

Jason held up his hand in a silent hush motion then, looking around he quietly said, "Or they've given up, hoping we will loosen up," he winked and continued. "Remain silent, we have to keep this secret."

Darce and Tetra both nodded and Darce added, "Perhaps they have a different plan. If they aren't concerned about our ability to use the SSSRD, they may be trying a new approach. A non-combative approach, perhaps a chemical attack, something that would kill all life on earth."

"I don't think so," said Jason. "These characters want to inhabit our planet as the prime species. That means moving billions of their people from here to Earth. A task that would take years, perhaps a hundred years or more." He paused, thinking then added, "They wouldn't want to destroy animal life or plant life, just human and not all at once—a phased attack that would take a hundred years."

"So, they kill us off a few at a time?" wondered Carsteen. "How would they accomplish that?"

"A military strike or series of strikes would meet with resistance and soon a major war," said Darce. "I think you're on to something here, Jason, but as the President said, how?"

"A slow process over a hundred years that wouldn't raise suspicion," said Carsteen, "as if we simply died off naturally."

"Sterilization," said Tetra. The three men looked at Tetra, "No new births," she reiterated.

* * *

Kalyx returned and secured himself. The shom lifted off and accelerated toward a large cylindrical structure at an altitude over eight-hundred kilometers above the planet's surface. The station was over three hundred meters in height and one hundred meters in diameter. There were four large doors stacked on one side of the structure, each about thirty meters by sixty-five meters. On the opposite side were four large docking bays and one was occupied.

Kalyx pointed toward the occupied docking bay and said, "The Kansat Kray, our transport is here."

Jason stared at the vessel, "Wow!" He was looking at a vessel that was over one hundred meters in length and twenty-five in diameter. The outer surface was metallic, black, and smooth. There were grey outlines indicating the locations of doors and alien lettering next to each door. The front of the vessel came to a flattened point and there were three main viewports stretched across the upper half of the nose through which a number of Dar'Wannians were visible, occupied at control panels similar to those on the bridge of the Karnis Tarb.

"This transport will take you to Dar'Fost," said Kalyx. "I will accompany you there and introduce you to someone there who will see to your needs." The shom moved to the large door opposite the transport and as it moved toward the door, it opened. The shom came to rest inside the station, the outer door closed and as the atmosphere was reintroduced into the bay, an inner door opened, and the three Earthlings were led into a large open area. Kalyx told the three, "Remain here, you may walk about, but stay close. We will be boarding the transport soon."

They gathered at a high table and tried to absorb the surroundings. The space was about seventy meters clear from the floor to the overhead structure and nearly seventy meters square. The docking bay door was open, and the interior of the transport vessel was visible. As they watched, a group of ten human women left the transport and were led to the bay where the shom was located. The doors were closed and secured, and the outer doors could be heard opening and the shom leaving. Then another craft was heard landing in the bay and the doors closed.

Carsteen whispered something to Tetra, she nodded, and he looked at the group. "Sterilization," he said quietly, "they may try to sterilize the entire planet and in a hundred years we'd be gone. Slowly and peacefully."

"Why do you say that?" asked Darce.

"Why would the women be going to the surface?" asked Tetra. "There are several possibilities and one of them is to be examined and experimented on. What other reason than for testing ways to sterilize them."

As Kalyx returned, Tetra stopped talking and the four were led aboard the transport. They were joined by several Dar'Wannian soldiers and a number of large fuel cells. Jason commented, "You could fit a baseball stadium in here." As he spoke, the loading bay door opened, and the Blue Wolf was brought aboard.

"Please secure yourselves," said Kalyx, "we are about to leave for the collection station."

"I thought we were going to Dar'Fost," said Darce.

"We are," said Kalyx, "but the collection station is on the way. We'll make a stop at that station to pick up more energy cells. This vessel uses a great amount of energy, and we make these trips as useful as possible."

Everybody was secured in a tilted pad and the transport slowly moved away from the space station and began a turn. Pointed in the right direction, the pilot advised all personnel the artificial gravity would be turned off during the trip to the collection station and the vessel moved forward gradually reaching its cruising speed. Three hours later another large structure was visible through the front view ports and the transport slowed. The transport moved slowly into docking position and as the securing clamps closed, the artificial gravity was again energized.

Kalyx returned and said, "We'll be here for several hours as the cells are loaded. You may leave the transport and walk about but be careful. The cells are not as strong as they appear. Each one holds a great deal of energy, and they are not to be played with. Now, I must verify the count with the station commander. I'll be back shortly."

Jason looked around and asked, "Kalyx, could I see the collection process and watch a concentration process?"

"There is not much to see, the process is very slow and there are not big machines grinding or pounding. If you wish to see stay with me," said Kalyx, "and I'll answer any questions I can, or I'm allowed to. Stay close."

As they passed a group of workers removing a large energy cell from a machine, Jason asked, "is that an energy collector?"

"The entire structure on that side is the collector and concentrator," said Kalyx. "That device is the fuel cell filler."

"Is that dangerous?" asked Jason, "Working with all that stored energy?"

"Yes, it is very dangerous," said Kalyx, "these workers are very well trained and even then, we have an occasional accident."

"Like an explosion?" wondered Jason aloud.

"No, not yet, hopefully not ever," said Kalyx. "If a container were to break open it could easily detonate and destroy this entire facility so, we are very careful. That is why we store them on Dar'Fost."

"How many stations like this are there?" asked Jason.

"Two," returned Kalyx. "But all fully charged cells are stored on Dar'Fost. It is much safer that way."

"Just how much energy is stored on Dar'Fost right now?" asked Jason.

"I don't know, enough for the planet to operate for the next year and for several vessels to operate."

"How long did it take to collect all this energy?" asked Jason.

"Once this facility was completed, it went quickly, less than half the full year," replied Kalyx.

"Is this a new facility?"

"Yes, we needed it to replace the original facility that was beginning to experience problems. It still functioned but could not produce enough to meet our needs. Now that this facility is almost fully functional, we have started to finish planning another new one and dismantle the original."

* * *

As the captives met aboard the transport vessel, they gathered to talk, "How would they sterilize the entire world?" asked Jason, "How?"

"Something airborne, or through the water supplies or both," said Tetra.

"You know, Mabosh was helping me as we repaired the Blue Wolf," said Jason. "I wonder if they may wish to use it to spread something around the Earth. The Wolf wouldn't raise any concerns as an alien vessel would."

"We have to be careful with these characters," said Carsteen. "How many lies do you think we have been told thus far? Do you think we're going back to Earth, or will they kill us when we've been drained of all we know?"

Jason grinned, "So, we tell 'em more lies. Like, there are really two or three versions of the SSSRD. Only one would be a WMD."

"Something, perhaps three or more units that will be placed in space between the Martian and Earth orbits … soon," said Carsteen, "and may not allow alien craft into our solar system ..."

"The Dar'Wannians have already been in Earth orbit in a threatening fashion and their probes have flown in and out. We should say that our SSSRD is in the final phases of testing, and should be ready for deployment, even as we speak," said Darce.

*   *   *

FOURTEEN

2246.03.06.08.36 (Off-World)   On Planet Dar'Fost

As the transport approached Dar'Fost the planet's surface came into view. It was another blue, green and brown orb surrounded by clouds. The transport assumed a high orbit and approached the planet's space station. Secured in place, the artificial gravity activated, Kalyx approached the Earthlings, "Your Blue Wolf is designed to fly in Earth's upper atmosphere, and therefore, it should be capable in this atmosphere as well."

Tetra looked at Kalyx, "Gravity, air density, other considerations, I wouldn't want to venture out in this planet's atmosphere without checking everything first."

"We've done all that," said Kalyx, "we've flown here many times in our Cains and in your Earth's atmosphere. I assure you, it's perfectly safe."

"Will you fly down with us?" asked Jason.

"Of course," returned Kalyx. "The power for the Wolf is being provided by the energy cell I placed in the conversion unit and all systems have responded like new."

Darce looked at his companions, they then nodded in unison, "Okay, we'll do it."

Kalyx looked at the four Earthlings, "You understand you are prisoners. The same conditions apply here as do on Dar'Wan, you have the freedom to walk about knowing there is no place to go, or to escape. You will encounter other humans captured in the taking of one of your space stations and they also have the freedom to wander about. Understand, we do not take care of our prisoners, they are placed here on Dar'Fost because there is no other place for them to go. They will survive on their own skills. They may trade work for food and building materials, but you are to be self-sufficient."

"What about food, shelter ...?" asked Carsteen.

"Over the last several hundred years, we have visited your planet numerous times," said Kalyx. "We have brought back various plants and animals. The animals are now wild, there are cattle, deer, pigs and even fish in the waters. There are also shelters we have constructed for ourselves, that are now occupied by your people and our criminals. The planet is quite inhabitable."

* * *

The trip down to the planet surface was uneventful. Kalyx directed Darce pointing to a large island in the middle of a very wide ocean. "We have chosen this location because it is not accessible from any of the land areas where we have located prisoners," said Kalyx. "The human prisoners are located here temporarily until we prepare another permanent location."

The Blue Wolf handled well and maneuvered in the atmosphere as it had on Earth. The island where they landed was a warm, dry, wide-open space with several low-rise buildings in a cluster and a low mountain range that seemed to run the entire perimeter of the island. The Blue Wolf stood out as the only craft of its kind amongst a dozen other crafts.

"Is this an airport?" asked Jason.

Kalyx thought for a moment, "Ah, an airport. I suppose it would be," he returned. "There are several such places on this planet, and we visit them as we bring in new prisoners. We keep the population as scattered about as we can, but this is the main port of entry." He looked up at the sky where the space station should be, "The space station is in a fixed orbit directly above this island." He picked up his communicator and said he would be occupied with off-loading the fuel cells and estimated a departure time in approximately four hours.

"You said there are criminals imprisoned here," said Darce. "Should we be concerned about our safety?"

"No," replied Kalyx, "the prisoner population is located on other islands, this island is our primary landing and control point, so no criminals here, just our staff, a small armed military presence and the members of your species."

Carsteen scanned the horizon, "I see mountains in the distance, how far are they from here?"

Kalyx did a mental calculation and replied, "I would estimate about fifteen kilometers and the distance to the ocean is between eighty and one hundred fifty kilometers, depending on which direction you choose."

"Where are the human prisoners?" asked Tetra.

"I really don't know," said Kalyx. "Many have remained near this control point; others have wandered off into the mountains or forests. They all have the freedom to go wherever they wish." He checked his communicator and continued, "If you plan to return to Dar'Wan, the transport will leave here on schedule. If you're not here, we assume you will stay." He turned and walked away.

Carsteen was visibly annoyed, he looked at his companions, "We are at war. These characters are planning on wiping out the human race and occupying the planet Earth. We have to do something."

"Mr. President," said Darce, "we are four, and on an alien planet...what do you propose?"

"I don't know, Captain. But as long as we're alive and able to move around, we look for anything, a weakness—something, anything that will give us the ability to keep them from attacking Earth."

"Well," said Jason, "we could blow up their energy collectors."

"How?" questioned Darce.

"Don't know," said Jason "... yet."

Darce looked at Carsteen, "Looks like we're going to knock out the energy collector."

"Then what?" asked Carsteen.

"They'll probably shoot us," said Darce.

"Yeah, true that," said Jason, "but no energy source means no trip to our little rock. The other energy station is taxed just powering their planet. It may take them years to get back up to speed, maybe a lotta years."

"Okay," said Carsteen, "let's find as many other humans as we can and start planning."

"Should we split up?" asked Tetra, "Meet back here in an hour and re-evaluate?"

"Agreed," said Carsteen. "I noticed a gathering of humans near those buildings." He pointed across the open area, "So, I'll go that way. Back here in an hour."

Carsteen approached a small gathering of humans. He was noticed by one of the people who said, "You're president Carsteen?"

"Yes," he answered, "and who are you?"

"Captain Janet Morrison, SW-13 chief medical officer."

"Doctor?" quizzed Carsteen.

'Yes sir," replied Morrison.

"Okay, Doctor, what's going on here?" asked Carsteen.

"We've been here for one hundred eleven of this planet's days and have been allowed complete freedom to wander," said Morrison. "We were told we would find an empty island with no criminals where we could make permanent homes and farm the land."

"How have they treated you?"

"They just started to sort us into groups that appear to be by age and gender," replied Morrison. "The older people are being sent away and the younger ones are being interviewed more intensely. Their interest seems to be primarily in women of childbearing age."

Carsteen nodded knowingly, "Okay, I understand. Now tell me, what happened? How did you get here?"

"We were on SW-13," replied Morrison, "the station was attacked and main sections severely damaged. All our fighters were lost. The total complement of 2,806 people was reduced to less than 1,800. Life support systems were down, and we were sheltering in place. They came aboard and took prisoners. We were loaded on to a massive transport and taken away. They blasted the station, killing anyone who may have been hiding."

"Where are they taking the women?" asked Carsteen.

"They take them to their main planet and give them physicals," responded Morrison, "complete physicals and they ask a lot of questions."

"Questions about what?"

"Mostly about reproduction," said Morrison. "Have you ever had children? Are you pregnant now? Have you tried to become pregnant and failed?"

"Why do you think they are asking those questions?" posed Carsteen.

"My impression," returned Morrison, "is they want to know how to sterilize the population being held here."

"I think it's bigger than that, Doctor, I think they want to sterilize our whole planet."

"To what end?" puzzled Morrison, "To get rid of all humans and have the planet for themselves?"

"That's exactly what they want," returned Carsteen.

"Much easier said than done," returned Morrison. "You'd have to deliver a sterilizing agent to every water source or spray every square inch of the inhabited world and even then, you'd miss someone. The whole thing would take years."

"I think they are planning on that exact scenario," said Carsteen, "when they get rid of enough humans, we become targets for military cleansing and sport for hunters."

"Can they do that? I mean, we're ten billion strong."

"They'd introduce the sterilization agents and keep it secret until a large portion of the population has been infected and then they'd move in with more direct tactics. We have to know what resources we have in people here. Do you have any staff?"

"Yes, my entire staff was captured." "What about others? Pilots? Technicians? Soldiers?" "Yes, some of each," returned Morrison.

"Keep a low profile and let your people know we are planning an escape. We're going to need everybody's cooperation if we're to get off this rock and back to Earth."

* * *

Jason had gone in the same direction as Kalyx and saw people, humans moving fuel cylinders to a shuttle. He walked over to a man moving a cylinder, "Hey, what are you doing?"

"Who are you?" asked the man.

"Name's Jason Leary, Sergeant, tech, who are you?"

"Frank Linsman, Lieutenant navigator and part-time pilot."

"Okay Lieutenant, did you watch as these characters drove that big transport?"

"Tried, but couldn't get close to the control panels," said Linsman.

"What about the shuttle," posed Jason, "could you get a better look?"

"Yeah," returned Linsman, "they only used a few controls, and they were fairly straightforward."

"I suggest you keep your eyes wide open on any future trips. We may want to borrow one or two of those little shuttles."

Linsman smiled, "You and who else?"

"You, if you want to take a shot at getting outta here," said Jason. "What about the rest of our people?"

"Well, they brought y'all here in a transport," returned Jason, "I'm thinkin' we might borrow one. Get everybody on board and take it for a joy ride ... home."

"You and me?" quizzed Linsman, "Anybody else?"

"Jacob Carsteen," said Jason.

"The President. He's here?"

"Yeah, we were on SW-27, and they let all but thirty or forty people use the escape pods to get to the surface," said Jason. "Condition was the President had to be taken prisoner, so the four of us were taken aboard their vessel."

"Four? Who else?"

"Major Tetra Harmon, and Captain Darce Gannon."

"Gannon's here?" blurted Linsman. "I know him."

"Okay so, what are you doing here?" asked Jason.

"We're still trying to figure any possible ways of getting outta here and back home."

"I don't know, they just told us to load these things on the shuttle and take 'em up to the transport vessel."

"They're concentrated energy cells. Have you been up there?" asked Jason.

"Yeah, I made the last trip up to offload."

"How many of these cylinders are on the transport now?" asked Jason.

"I don't know, about twenty, maybe more."

"You're a navigator, could you find your way back to our planet if you had control of that big transport?" asked Jason.

"Navigator and sometime pilot. I was part of a backup crew for a tach bird. I never got a chance to get in the fight and all our birds were lost. So, yeah, give me a shot at the control panel and I'd give it a ride, at least outta here—hopefully home."

"How many more like you are there, navigators and pilots who may have another piece of the control puzzle?"

"A few, maybe a dozen."

"Find 'em and bring 'em in to meet with us at the control center but do it quietly. We don't want to raise any suspicion amongst the bad guys."

*   *   *

Darce encountered several Dar'Wannian soldiers patrolling the area around the airport. Each was carrying a hollow tube weapon. In total, he counted fifty-four soldiers, usually in pairs, never alone. He wandered less than a mile from the control center and turned back. As he was walking, he met three soldiers and greeted them. "Hi, guys." He said thinking they couldn't understand him.

To his surprise, one of the soldiers returned the greeting, "Hi, how are you?"

"You speak English?" asked Darce.

"Not very well," said the soldier. "I am to be more trained in your language but have not been to your planet yet. Most of us were sent here to assist in communication with your people near the control center and become more familiar with your language."

"What's your name?" asked Jason.

"Voast," replied the soldier.

Darce saw an opportunity to gain more information, "So, will you be going to Earth?"

"When the time is right, I think many of us will go," said Voast.

"In that transport at the space station?" quizzed Darce.

"The Mulbor Kray, maybe," said Voast, "there are two such vessels that could make the trip. The Mulbor and the Kansat."

"I saw them unloading energy cells after we arrived," said Darce. "I wonder how many cells they will need to make the trip to earth and back."

"The Mulbor Kray, the large one would need twice as many cells as the smaller one, the Kansat Kray, the smaller one can only take about a thousand troops so, I would guess the larger vessel."

"Then, maybe both could go," said Darce.

"I do not think so," said Voast, "the Kansat is in need of repairs, and we will still need that energy here and on Dar'Wan. It will take a long time to build up our reserves enough to repair the vessel and make another transporter trip."

As they approached the control center, Darce said, "it was nice talking to you, see you around." He left the soldiers and returned to the place where he was to meet with Carsteen, Tetra and Jason.

* * *

"What have we learned?" asked Carsteen.

"We need to know more about the control of the transport vessels. Lieutenant Linsman can gather some of that info from the people here on the ground. Jason and I will take as many trips on the Mulbor Kray as we can and observe."

"So, you're planning on stealing the Mulbor to make an escape?" quizzed Carsteen.

"Stealing?" echoed Jason, "No, we're just going to borrow it for a few days. Take a joy ride."

"Yeah," added Darce, "for about twenty lightyears."

"I'll stay here with our people," said Carsteen. "We need to know how many are here and how many are past the mountains and beyond."

Darce, Tetra and Jason returned to the Blue Wolf and found Kalyx talking to several of his people. "Are you going back up to your transport?" asked Darce.

"Yes," returned Kalyx. "Did you want to return to Dar'Wan?"

"Yes," replied all three.

"We thought you might be more comfortable here," said Kalyx. "It is so much more like your home planet."

"True that," said Jason, "but I like to fly and see the stars." Darce added, "We all do."

* * *

The Mulbor departed on time and the trio of Earthlings were on board watching everything they could, standing close to various control panels and asking questions about the stars as they came into view. At the same time Carsteen was meeting with groups of the people on Dar'Fost, swearing them to absolute secrecy and determining who had scattered toward and beyond the mountains.

Lieutenant Linsman brought together twenty-five technicians, each who had observed something on their voyage from Earth and also from Dar'Wan to Dar'Fost. As a group, they compiled a very rough manual of operation for the transport.

Conversations continued into various scenarios for making their escape.

"We may have to overpower the soldiers, even kill some of them," offered one of the humans.

"We'll need enough energy cells," said another.

"We have to get past the Cains," was a comment from several at once.

"Does the transport have weapons?" asked one of the women.

"We'll need food and water for the trip home," said another.

"We'll have very little time to get out of range of their weapons."

"And their Cains."

The planning went on well into the night and the next day. Carsteen had taken several power naps and was ready for more plotting when light broke over the horizon. "Korta, I believe that's what they call the star. It's so much like our sun; I could almost get used to it here."

Food was brought in, and the conversations were gaining intensity as two soldiers approached, "We are looking for Darce Gannon," said one of the soldiers. "Is he here?"

"No," replied Carsteen, "He's gone back to Dar'Wan."

"Jason Leary?" questioned the soldier.

"Dar'Wan," said Carsteen.

"Tetra Harmon?"

"She went with them."

"And you Mr. President."

Carsteen stood and the soldiers ushered him out of the building and across the open area to the control building. A door opened and Marshall came out to meet Carsteen. "Mr. President, we have arranged for you and your companions to remain here at this control center. I trust the accommodations will meet with your approval. Please follow me."

Carsteen was led to a square, four-story building with large windows and balconies on the top floor. The entrance was guarded by two Dar'Wannian soldiers outside and the door was secured with controlled locks. The door opened to a three-meter-wide hall about three meters long ending with a second door and two more soldiers. Beyond the second door, the interior opened to a square room about twelve meters on a side with nine square meter offices on the perimeter.

"The fourth level is your suite," said Marshall. "Your companions will each have a suite on the third level and the second is a kitchen and dining area.

This first level is a meeting hall and administrative offices where you may govern the human population."

"Actually, Marshall, we had hoped to be returning to Earth and all this would be unnecessary."

"No, Mr. President, you and the others here on Dar'Fost will remain permanently," said Marshall. "Please understand, we do not care if you or your people live or die. You are given this planet and several resources as an act of civility. This is now your home as it will be for any other humans taken prisoner in this struggle."

* * *

FIFTEEN

2246.03.22.16.21 (Off-World) Aboard the Mulbor Kray

Aboard the Mulbor Kray, Jason, Tetra and Darce were watching the operation as closely as they could. Darce wandered to the main pilot's station, "This is amazing, guiding this vessel through the maze of asteroids, stars and planets, how you do it at the elevated speeds is beyond me."

"The navigation system handles most of the smaller objects," replied the pilot, "we can steer closer to or farther from stars and use their gravity as we wish. This is an energy-conserving choice and must be done very carefully."

"I thought the energy in the fuel cells was more than enough to travel between the stars," said Tetra.

"The travel between Dar'Wan and Dar'Fost does not require such manipulation, but the journey to Earth would consume nearly twice the energy if we did not use the gravitational forces of stars as we pass them," said the pilot.

"How much energy did you use in coming to Earth in this transport?" asked Tetra.

"I believe we used four large energy packs on the voyage to Earth and another seven on the return to Dar'Wan," said the pilot. "The weight on the return voyage was considerably greater."

As Jason stood near another controller, he was asked, "What interests you?"

"The stars," replied Jason. "I have observed them from Earth and the several stations in our system. This is a completely new point of observation…fascinating."

"In order to travel amongst the stars, one must learn them from many points," said the controller.

"I see that," replied Jason. "I think my first question should be about my star, where is it in this mass of little lights?"

The pilot touched his screen and the main view screen changed images to a wide view of space. On the right side of the view screen he circled a small cluster of stars. "Your star and your planet are here," he said. "Your system of measurement would place it about twenty lightyears away from our system. If we were to travel there, we would use several other stars as gravity anchors to increase speed or slow us down. The shortest distance to Earth is not a straight line."

Jason studied the star pattern and at the same time memorized the several touches the controller made to energize the view screen. As the trip to Dar'Wan continued, Darce and Jason continued to watch and question the crew about the control of the ship and the stars they could see.

* * *

Back on Dar'Fost, Carsteen was given a tour of the interior of the building that was proposed as his quarters. The building had two main staircases, one on each side and no elevator.

"We never had a use for elevators and four levels are not that difficult to ascend," said Marshall.

The Mulbor Kray returned to Dar'Fost and the Blue Wolf was again shuttled to the surface. Jason looked at Darce, "A good trip?"

"Definitely," responded Darce. "What little bits did you gather?"

"Spotting our star and manipulating the main view screen," said Jason, "You?"

"A few more control features. I wanted to ask about increasing speed to the LS+4 level, but that would have been pushing our luck."

"I wandered the large cargo area and saw fourteen weapon stations. It appears the tubes the soldiers carry are also used in these stations. Apparently, the tube is inserted in a slot and the soldier controls his tube. I think at maximum power, one of these tubes could take down a Cain."

* * *

"Welcome back," said Carsteen. "We're now being housed in new quarters," he said pointing at the square, grey building. "You each get an apartment on the third floor, and I get the fourth. The second floor is a kitchen and dining area. The first floor is for administrative functions. That gives us a venue in which we can comfortably talk to our people."

"That's your new White House?" said Darce.

Carsteen laughed, "Yeah, quite a comedown."

"Looks more like a grey cube than a white house," said Jason.

"Whatever it is or isn't, it's now our headquarters," said Carsteen. "So, let's get busy and call the next meeting with the other people on this island."

"In small groups?" quizzed Darce.

"Yes, in lots of fifty or sixty at a time," said Carsteen.

"When do we start?" asked Jason.

"Now," said Carsteen, "The first topic is spreading the word that we're here and the planning has begun. We have to contact everybody, no matter how far they've wandered."

They looked around at the immediate area, buildings, trees and low rolling hills in the distance all looked promising places to find other humans. They went in different directions, planning on being back in an hour to again coordinate and expand their search. They each found several people who responded with enthusiasm and each of them went out to their own circle of friends, bringing the total number of people who attended the next meeting to over sixty. After a brief initial discussion, all sixty reached out to more of the population. As higher-ranking military types were found, they were asked to come directly to the 'Cube' for more detailed discussion.

Carsteen remained in the cube trying to organize the leadership structure for the hundreds and perhaps thousands of humans. As he was writing down his thoughts the door opened and someone in a dark hooded cloak entered. "Mr. President," queried the individual.

"Yes," returned Carsteen as he looked up at the dark figure. "And who are you?" he asked.

"My name is Rowclay," returned the figure as he removed his hood revealing a gray, almost human face. His hands were large with long thin fingers. His eyes were oval in shape, his nose wide and flat and his mouth small but his speech was perfect English and his voice was deep, "I am of the Talmonoria and mean you no harm."

"The Talmonoria," Carsteen puzzled, "and you speak our language."

"Yes," returned Rowclay, "also Dar'Wannian and several other languages. I learned English before making my first visit to your planet."

"You've been to Earth?"

"Yes, a most interesting place, your Earth. The various ethnic groups, languages, cultures and varieties of people. Your differing political backgrounds, art, literature and science ...I find it more interesting at each visit."

"Are you part of this business?" asked Carsteen. "Kidnapping us and holding us prisoner while our planet is taken over?"

"No, Jacob, your species and the Dar'Wannians have both demonstrated value in our vision of the larger universe," said Rowclay. "We had hoped this meeting of the two races would lead to the sharing of ideas and cooperative ventures in finding and settling new worlds."

"So, you led them to us and are about to let them take our planet and wipe out our race."

"We normally do not interfere in the contests between civilizations but ... there are exceptions. We have watched your planet and the Dar'Wannians' planet for thousands of your years and value you both. The coming collision of several planets in both galaxies has threatened that vision. We cannot change the courses of the planets, so the collision will occur. Our solution was to encourage development of the Dar'Wannians' travel capabilities and guide them to explore other worlds. They found Earth and unfortunately, have used those capabilities to attempt to conquer Earth and threaten the continuation of your race."

Carsteen shook his head, looked at Rowclay and said, "Then why don't you simply make them stop their aggressive moves?"

"We have a military capability that could easily force them to stop but they would resist, and the outcome would be devastating to the Dar'Wannians. We'd rather try to stay out of the dispute process between the worlds and races we encounter. Our interference here is intended to even the balance between you both, not advantage one over the other. You will still have some sort of conflict and many lives may be lost but we hope both races will survive and continue. Perhaps, over time, you will become allies, cooperating in further exploration and settling of this galaxy as well as others in the universe."

"Others?"

"The Andromeda soon will not be out of your reach as you learn how to use different forms of energy and materials and move between the various dimensions over the next few hundred years."

"Are you talking about wormholes?" asked Carsteen.

"You have much to learn," replied Rowclay. "You must open your minds, question everything and reach out into the unknown. We are confident you will learn."

"When will we be able…?" began Carsteen.

"It may take generations," said Rowclay, "but remember as one of your philosophers said long ago, '*every journey begins with a single step.*'"

"What will we find in the Andromeda?" wondered Carsteen.

"I have told you enough for now," said Rowclay, "remember, reach out into the unknown."

"So, are you here to tease me with these treasures?"

"I am here to encourage you in your escape from this planet and return to Earth. I may advise you during your journey as necessary to guide you back to Earth but the conflict between the two populations must be resolved without our further involvement."

"What should we do next?"

Rowclay smiled, "Reach out, take the next step." Then he turned, pulled the hood up over his head, walked out through the door and vanished into the darkness.

* * *

Two days later the final group of sixty-four people was assembled in the Cube's first-floor meeting space. The building was searched for listening devices and none were found. Jason identified twelve people, some with military experience, to serve as security guards at the doors and as lookouts.

The conversations were about organizing the entire population into military-like units that could overpower the Dar'Wannian soldiers, take their weapons, and seize the transport vessel. "We don't have weapons that would allow overpowering them from a distance so, we'll have to do this up close and very personal," said Jason. "Everyone should have some kind of blade, one that can be easily hidden on yourself and still big enough to kill." He showed the gathering a piece of metal he had fashioned into a dagger. "Important parts, the blade, the grip or hilt and the cross-guard. When you make a dagger don't forget the cross-guard, it will keep your hand from sliding up onto the blade. Make the blade sharp enough to slit your enemy's throat."

Darce added, "Each team looking at a target should all agree ahead of time, someone will grab the head, someone grab the tube, someone get the powerpack off his wrist someone grab his ankles so he can't move about, someone grab his other arm and whoever is left, hold him down."

Jason continued, "I know you are not trained assassins, but you each have to act like one. Killing may be totally against what you believe in, but this is war, and we have no other option."

"Don't hesitate to use your daggers," said Darce, "remember, these characters attacked us and wouldn't hesitate to use those tube things on us."

One of the people listening to Jason and Darce stood and approached Darce, "Captain, my name is Connor Brinkman, and I can show these people what to do, how to take down a soldier."

Tetra entered the space and approached Brinkman, "Sergeant, good to see you again."

"Major Harmon," returned Brinkman, "how have you been?"

"No more bumps and bruises from your training sessions. Now it's all cuts and scratches from working on my hobby."

Tetra looked at Darce, "Listen to this one, Darce, he knows his stuff."

"You have some experience, Sergeant?" asked Darce.

"Name's Connor Brinkman, and yes sir, eight years in a special-forces strike unit," said the Sergeant. "Intensive training back on the surface for six years and I rarely had to use it."

"Well then Connor, how do you propose we proceed?" asked Darce.

"Well sir, I was sent up to this station to run the fitness program and decided to offer some hand combat lessons as an alternative to pushups and jumping jacks."

"First;" said Connor, "we keep this as quiet as possible; they have to think we're resigned to living here on Dar'Fost and we're happy.

"Second, we have to define all the potential targets and assign a five or six-man team of people to take on each one. We may have enough people to assign multiple teams to various targets. These teams will have to have a plan of attack that includes killing the aliens.

"Third, we have to practice the attack procedure as often as we can and make it a muscle memory action. We can't have anyone backing down or not slicing deep enough.

"Fourth, we have to have a means of communication so we can coordinate the time of the attacks both here on the ground and on the space station."

"So, we need a count of all possible targets," said Carsteen. "Then we can divide our people into teams. We should identify as many people with military experience as we can and spread the talent around."

"We probably have a near-twenty-to-one ratio advantage over the bogies," said Jason, "so we may be able to have two teams of four to six people assigned to each target."

"This is war," said Carsteen, "as much as I detest violence, there is no other way. We can't take prisoners and guard them, we'll have to kill the soldiers, take their weapons, disable the transport vehicles we don't need, and destroy their communications systems. Once we begin, there will be no turning back. We kill the soldiers, contain the worker population, load the Shoms with our people and all the energy containers and get on board the transport vessel as quickly as possible."

"When we leave the planet, all means of space transportation must be left inoperable," said Darce.

Carsteen continued, "Let's begin now, counting the targets and our own people. Connor, I suggest you find as many people as you can who can follow your lead and pass on the training to the groups then check on them and keep us all on the same page.

Connor moved through the immediate crowd, speaking in a low voice and selecting a number of individuals to take leadership roles. He found twenty-seven current and former military people who all had experienced his training on the surface or on SW-23. These group leaders were told, "This is a black-ops-type mission. We capture and kill. There is no room for mercy or holding prisoners. If any other Dar'Wannians get in the way, the same applies…kill."

Connor described the best way to quickly eliminate targets. He started with teams of four to six people each with a specific task. "In each group, one of you will have to be the prime blade, the one who will deliver the killing thrust to the soldier. You can't hesitate, when there's an opening, you must strike, hard and fast. Plunge as deep as you can and twist the blade, doing as much damage as you can." He studied the group noticing some looks of confusion, "Remember, these beings have already killed thousands of our people, it is now us or them. Kill and don't think about it."

"What do we do then?" asked one.

"Be sure the soldier is dead, take his tube and armband as well as any communicators he has, and get to the Cube. We will be loading up cargo shuttles for a trip to the large transport."

"Are you sure we have to kill?" asked another.

Connor reiterated, "Yes, this is war, people."

Tetra added, "There is no other way, now. Let's get started."

* * *

Darce gathered two separate groups of pilots, navigators, and spacecraft technicians. Their task would be to take the work already done by Linsman and his group, add to or massage the content to complete an operation manual of the transport. Then be ready to fly it back to their solar system in the Milky Way. Jason, Tetra and Darce met with each group and relayed the information gathered in their several voyages on Dar'Wannian craft. Six astrophysicists wandered between the two groups offering their expertise to the teams.

Each group was to secure food and water for the voyage. It was assumed the trip would take at least five days, perhaps more if they weren't comfortable with the extreme speeds.

A complement of thirty-four enemy soldiers was counted and assigned two of the teams. Each team then assigned one of their people to track the soldier's movements and the two watchers worked together. There were another eighteen ground personnel and an unknown number of workers on the space station. The two pilot/navigator teams would address the space station personnel.

"Talk to the soldiers, learn as much as you can about their daily habits," said Darce, "we want to know when they are most vulnerable. Also, learn all you can about their weapons. Ask if we can have some sort of hunting weapon to pursue deer."

Jason learned that the tube weapons could be adjusted to deliver various intensities of energy. "A high setting would obliterate a cow," said Voast, "making it absolutely useless and at the same time drain the power pack worn on the arm. The tube and the armband are a pair, no mixing of tubes and armbands would work, so a tube could not be used without the related armband. The higher settings are for leveling walls or moving dirt. In hunting deer or cattle, you should use one of the lower settings, perhaps the second for a large deer and the first for a small deer."

"I think I understand," said Jason as he noticed the matching symbols on both components, "but I'd like to see it working."

"We are due to spend time at our practice site today," said Voast. "You could accompany us if you like."

*   *   *

The practice site was an open area that seemed to stretch to the distant mountains. There were numerous posts scattered about at various distances from the firing line, some with objects balanced on top. There were also boulders the size of three or four men, and swinging targets suspended from beams.

The soldiers all adjusted the settings on the controllers on their arms, pointed their weapons at a target and began firing. The energy blast was in the form of small streaks of light that were accompanied by a crack like thunder and struck the targets with a burst of light. "We are on low settings," said Voast, "we will increase the energy level as we continue, but never to the maximum. Such a discharge would be deafening and very dangerous." He pointed the tube at a target citing which one he was aiming at and squeezed the thick part of the tube. The flash of energy left the tube and struck the target almost instantaneously. "It moves at the speed of light," said Voast. "And it moves in a straight line." He made an adjustment on his arm and said, "The green square out there," pointing at a target about two hundred yards away as he again squeezed the tube. The sound was louder, the flash brighter and the green target disappeared.

"Was that the high setting?" asked Jason.

Voast pointed at a small blue square in front of a boulder another hundred yards farther away, "No, and this next one will still be at less than 25% power," he looked at the others on the firing line and shouted something in their language. All others stopped their firing and watched as Voast carefully aimed his tube at his target and squeezed the tube. The burst of light formed a thin, straight line from tube to target and the shock wave cracked like a clap of thunder as the target was obliterated and the boulder was struck, turning it to bits of gravel and dust. Voast looked at Jason, "25% power."

Jason's thought went immediately to the imaginary SSSRD he and Darce had joked about, *This damn thing would fit the bill as one,* he thought. He looked at Voast and with a small grin, nodded "Impressive," as if he had seen such weaponry before.

*   *   *

During the next meeting at the Cube, Carsteen suggested that the groups of fifty or sixty select a leader to attend meetings and relay information back to the groups. "We can't have hundreds of people gathering at the Cube every day. The team approach will have thirty to forty people—leaders, visiting the cube. Your team leaders can come and go at random times so as not to raise suspicion."

Darce found six other pilots and navigators who would form the core of the piloting crews aboard the Mulbor. He formed four complete crews, "Each crew will be six hours on and eighteen hours off. We have to remain as alert and well-rested as we can." The discussions touched on various scenarios and Darce reminded each group, "We want to be ready to move as soon as we can and be ready to push the buttons and flip the levers. There will be no time to ponder the control panels. Be ready to act as soon as we're aboard."

The emphasis shifted to people, fuel, food, and water. "We have to get all our people ready to board the shoms at a moment's notice," said Darce, "people will have to be close, hidden—but close."

"You mentioned fuel," said Frank Linsman, "what do you propose?"

"First we will need several large cylinders for the trip home," returned Darce, "I would guess at least four, but allowing for errors in navigation and slower speeds due to our lack of experience with the vessel, I'd double that number."

"Eight," said Linsman. "Shouldn't be a problem to locate that many and have them ready to load on a shom. If I can suggest, why not take as many as we can...don't leave any for the bad guys to use against us."

"Agreed," said Darce. "Now for food and water, we should have enough for the entire complement of about eighteen-hundred people for five or six days, more if possible."

Jan Morrison stood, "I'll take that on. That and any medical needs."

* * *

SIXTEEN

2246.03.27.14.07 (Off-World) Dar'Fost

The ground-based strike teams all rehearsed a seize and kill scenario. When the time came, they would have less than a minute to take down their targets. Sessions stressed a kill, not just a disabling strike, but a kill. At least three knives were to be used striking the throat, the heart and the back of the neck. No matter which escape scenario was adopted, the soldiers had to be eliminated first.

As the strike teams prepared for the attack, the piloting/navigation groups spent several hours each day wandering about the control area, asking questions about the various space-capable craft and traveling in hyperspace.

Darce, Jason and Tetra had wandered the island several times, observing the Dar'Wannian behavior, counting Dar'Wannian personnel, asking innocent questions and thinking about various escape plans. They had the core group of four meeting at the Cube for another brainstorming session, each with more input.

"The only possible escape would involve seizing the Mulbar Kray," said Carsteen. "The Kansat is not near ready for flight in hyperspace." The team was in agreement, and he continued, "The four of us will remain above the minutia, delegate everything you can and let the people do their work. We don't have time to waste on micro-managing each task."

"Agreed," said Tetra, "I've got Brinkman handling the individual assault groups."

Darce added, "I've got Lieutenant Linsman organizing the pilots and navigators into four groups, each capable of handling the operation of the transport on the trip home."

Jason said the food and water collection was being handled by Dr. Morrison as well as the regular medical needs. "I also have a few guys locating energy cells ready to load when the time is right."

"Okay," said Carsteen. "Now, what about the population that has gone farther out into the woods or beyond the mountains?"

"I'd like to try something," said Darce. "If I can suggest to the Dar'Wannians that I'd like to notify all our people about the presence of the president for everybody's benefit and the Blue Wolf is down for serious repairs." He paused, grinned and continued, "Perhaps I could use one of their Cains or a Tarb."

"They may say yes to your suggestion, but I'd be surprised if they allowed you to fly it alone," said Carsteen.

"No worries," said Jason, "let one of their people go with you. As far as they are concerned, you're there to contact people, not to fly their damn Cain and you can question every control feature, one pilot to another."

"Who knows?" said Carsteen, "They may just let you drive."

"One more thing," said Tetra, "I'm going to tell Brinkman to constantly remind the strike teams that these characters have already killed thousands of humans."

"Yes, let the hate build," said Carsteen, "it'll make the killing much easier."

* * *

The next several days were spent training, observing the operation of the various vessels, and contacting the people who had wandered afield. After a full week, Tetra reported to the group, "The strike teams are all prepped, they're ready now if we need, but each day makes them a little better."

"The piloting crews are gaining confidence," said Darce, "we've been building a manual that we think will get us home. It's still a long shot."

"It's a distance of 20 lightyears," said Jason. "We'd be moving at the Dar'Wannian speeds of LS+4. You realize that's over nine-trillion kilometers per hour, and we've never flown above a million kilometers per hour. This is absolutely crazy."

"Agreed," said Tetra, "I've had several conversations with the astrophysicists and traveling in hyperspace is scary as hell, but it's the only way home."

"You have a better idea?" asked Darce.

Jason raised his eyebrows and shrugged, "Nope, if we don't do this, our planet and everybody on it will be taken over by these characters, so let's get started."

Casteen said, "I've heard there's a transport due here in the next few days."

"Do we know which one?" asked Darce. "The Mulbar could transport all our people, the Kansat couldn't, and it's in need of repairs."

"We'll see when it arrives," said Carsteen. "Keep in mind, these Dar'Wannians want to take over the entire Earth and they want to start now—we don't have the luxury of time. We have to move as soon as possible. Are you three sure we're ready for this?"

"Ready? Hell no! We'll keep up the prep work until the opportunity presents and give it our best shot," returned Darce. "Let's get the ball rolling."

"Okay, so we seize the Mulbar, then what?" asked Jason. "You know they'll come after us immediately."

"That they will," returned Darce. "First, we keep this as quiet as possible, they have to think we're resigned to living here on Dar'Fost and we're happy. We have to be everywhere at once, so we count the bogies, locate each one and have a crew assigned to keep them under surveillance and be ready to take them down simultaneously. We have to be on the ground and up at the station when we move and don't allow any communication with Dar'Wan. We knock out the ground and station military first, then we have to get all the working personnel, neutralize them and get our people up to the station. Once the people, fuel, food and water are on board and we have pulled away from the station, we destroy the collection and concentration facility with one or two nukes and hope all the Cains are on board and damaged beyond use in the process."

"What about the Karnis Tarb and its Cains," asked Carsteen.

"I'm not sure where it is right now," said Darce, "Jason and I will be aboard the Blue Wolf. We'll take a turn around the station and look for any stray craft that could hinder progress. Anything that could stop us, we'll take out. As soon as the Mulbor is ready to begin its acceleration, we'll get back on board and secure the Wolf."

"It's our best shot," said Carsteen.

* * *

As the Mulbor Kray moved into docking position at the station and the connections were being secured, Carsteen was notified that a delivery of essentials for the humans had arrived. He was told to bring a crew of his people to load the supplies onto a cargo shuttle and take them down to the surface.

"This may be our best opportunity to act," said Carsteen. "Are all the strike teams ready to move?"

"Now is as good a time as any," said Jason. "We'll probably need some time to get the full teams in position, but I'll do a check on the teams and if its looking good, we'll do a green light countdown."

Carsteen contacted Darce, "The light may turn green. Let's start the process."

The tree was activated, Darce contacted the leads of the four pilot/navigator teams, Tetra found Brinkman still working with two strike teams and Jason found his three prime contacts. All teams were shortly notified and began moving toward the control center and their targets. The leaders assembled in the Cube where Carsteen began to address those present.

"I'll take our pilot/navigator teams up on the pretext of unloading our supplies," said Darce. He looked at Tetra, "Is the Wolf ready to fly?"

"It is," returned Tetra, "I'll have the missile tubes loaded and Jason and I will bring it up as soon as you've cleared the deck."

Connor Brinkman approached Darce, "Captain, I'd like to be with your strike team attacking the transport vessel."

"Wouldn't you be better here on the ground with all these teams?"

"Captain, when we were being transported here, I saw several of the guards putting their tube weapons into small round slots below view ports along the vessel's side. I think these are a part of their transports defense and we have to be aware of them and may be able to use them."

"Part?" speculated Darce.

"Sure, a vessel that size would have some major weaponry."

Darce checked in with the Control Center, "We're here to go up to the station and unload the supplies."

"Ah, Captain Gannon," said the soldier, "yes, I was told to expect an unloading team." He looked at the gathering of over fifty people, "Are you sure you need all these people to unload the materials?"

Darce laughed and looked at the gathered group, "Probably not, but I'm in a hurry and these people don't work very fast. Better to have too many, than too few."

The soldier laughed with Darce and said, "The shom, there," he said pointing at the closest cargo shuttle. "Your call sign will be 7629."

"Thanks, has someone been assigned to go with us?"

"I don't have anyone listed," said the soldier, "do you need help? I thought you were trained on these vehicles."

"Not a problem for me," returned Darce, "just let the station know I'll be coming."

The soldier laughed again, "I believe Commander Storgon can accompany you," he said as he lifted his communicator.

Storgon was an experienced command pilot. He boarded the shom and joined Darce in the control cabin as the full complement of fifty-four pilots and navigators came aboard the shom. "I am told you are a good pilot, Captain. Please take the controls and let the ground crew know you are the primary pilot."

Darce opened a link to the ground controller, "This is 7629 awaiting clearance."

"Noted 7629, bring your Shom to the release point there," said the ground controller as he pointed at the nearest launch circle.

Storgon watched closely as Darce manipulated the controls and maneuvered the Shom to the designated circle.

The complement of fifty-four pilots and navigators secured themselves in the cargo bay as Darce lifted off to the minimum maneuvering height, brought the shom around to the launch circle, and gently set it down. "7629 ready for lift off," he spoke into the com-link.

"7629, please lift to four meters above surface and move out to the launch circle directly ahead and hold."

"Aye, control, lifting off now," said Darce. "Altitude four meters."

"7629, you are cleared to lift to two kilometers and hold."

"Aye control, lifting to two kilometers."

Darce asked Storgon if he was doing the sequence correctly as he held the shom at the two-kilometer level until the control center cleared him for continued elevation to the station level.

Storgon nodded in approval.

"7629 you are now in the station's controlled area, Control Central out."

"7629, this is Station Control, do you copy?"

"This is 7629, and we copy, awaiting further instructions."

"Captain Gannon, please come to bearing 47, mark 0 and approach open bay door at speed factor 1. You will set down on the first circle."

"Copy that," said Darce. He brought the shom inside the station and set down on the deck.

"Well done, Captain, now release the cargo bay doors, here," said Storgon, pointing to a control lever.

Storgon remained with the shom, and Darce led his team of men off and was immediately met by a station coordinator. "Welcome aboard, Captain. Your materials are on board the Mulbor Kray through that door," he said pointing to the large opening opposite the door through which Darce had entered. "Your supplies are stacked inside; they are expecting you."

"Thank you," said Darce and looked at his group, "this way team."

The crew walked slowly across the open space, noticing all the personnel present and took special notice of weapons stacked neatly off to one side and the soldiers still wearing their armbands. They boarded Mulbor Kray and were met by another coordinator.

Darce opened his com-link to Carsteen, "Sir, the materials ready to load on a shom. Condition green plus four, unknown number of smaller packages, probably thirty plus."

Carsteen understood there to be four armed soldiers and about thirty other personnel. He immediately contacted Jason, "Darce checked in at green. What is your status?"

Jason requested a check down of each team pair. All teams checked in with only six red lights. "Six reds," he reported, "say when green," he spoke into his com-link. Within seconds three reds went green and Jason requested another read. Two minutes passed and finally the last of the reds went green.

"All targets are located and in range," said Carsteen. He verified Darce's status and said to both, "In three we are a go...two...one...GO!"

All strike teams hit their targets within seconds, both on the ground and in the space station. The ground teams of up to eight team members attacked the soldiers. First the soldiers were approached calmly as if there was no threat. Then when they were close enough, the humans rushed the soldier, grabbing his weapon and slashing a knife across his throat or plunging the blade into his body. Several soldiers were dead within seconds of the attack others fought furiously and inflicted damage on the humans before being subdued and killed.

The four soldiers on the station were each attacked by five or six humans and killed immediately. Their armbands were removed and paired with the appropriate tubes, then given to four selected humans with soldier backgrounds. The thirty-four station working personnel were gathered and secured aboard the shom. Storgon was restrained and kept as prisoner.

"Please tell your people to remain quiet and no one else will have to die," Darce told Storgon. "We just want to get home and have no interest in killing when not necessary." He looked at Frank Linsman, "Get your team started loading as many fuel cells as they can find and any food or water supplies on the station." He looked at Storgon and turned to Frank, "Please take our guest to the bridge and secure him there. We will have a need for his expertise during the voyage home and I'm sure he will prove useful." Darce then took the four armed men and the prisoners aboard the shom and returned to the planet's surface. "Jason we're landing in three minutes, what's your status?"

At the same time Darce and his crew were taking over the station, the ground teams were attacking their targets. Reports started immediately ... "Count down," said Jason.

"One: Clear." "Two: Clear." "Three ..." The numbers started coming in. At twenty-six there was a pause.

"Twenty-six ... status?" There was no response and Jason said, "Twenty-seven, check in."

"Twenty-seven: Clear," came the reply.

The count continued as Jason ran out of the Cube and toward the area where team twenty-six was located. He took a tube and armband. Coming out of the brush, Jason saw two soldiers, one standing over a body as he questioned a captured kneeling human. The other soldier held his weapon trained on the other humans from team twenty-six. The team was down, two were dead, three were injured and one was being questioned.

Jason didn't know which direction on the control was max and which was minimum. He placed the control near the mid-point, aimed his tube and fired as he ran, striking the soldier questioning the kneeling man. The blast was higher than necessary, and the soldier was ripped apart with bits and pieces of flesh, blood and bone splattering the ground. The second soldier turned, trying to bring his weapon up when Jason fired a second time. The second soldier was struck in his chest and suffered the same fate as his companion.

"Saddle up," said Jason, "grab their weapons and let's get back to the Cube." The three injured humans leaned on their friends so they could walk, and the two dead were carried. The team made it back to the Cube as another team reported having lost a man and taking out four Dar'Wannians.

The fighting had been furious, twelve humans were lost and another fourteen were injured, requiring medical attention.

All Dar'Wannian soldiers were down, most killed, others restrained, and all weapons were collected by the humans.

Carsteen approached Jan Morrison in the Cube tending to the injured humans, "Doctor, how are we looking?"

"All teams accounted for," replied Morrison. "There are twelve fatalities thus far," she said looking at the men stretched out in front of her. "I'm not sure how many of the remaining injured will make it home but my guess is that six probably won't make it home."

"Stand by, Doctor," said Carsteen, "this is far from over."

* * *

A Signal had been sent to Dar'Wan from the control center as the attacks began. The available craft capable of responding included three Tarb class vessels; the Karnis the Borster and the Enkar, along with their complement of six Cains each. The Karnis was in the middle of refueling and several minor repairs. The Borster was en route to Dar'Wan and would be in need of similar refueling and minor repairs. The Enkar had been refueled and all repairs were close enough to completion. It was deemed ready for full service. The Enkar's crew had been recalled and were ready to leave for Dar'Fost. The other two Tarbs would follow when ready, if necessary. The Karnis was put on a rush schedule and the replacement energy cell was at 75% after being installed. "It's the best we have, Commander," the maintenance tech told Hylak.

"Are there no other energy cells here?" posed Hylak.

"None" returned the tech. "They have been moved to Dar'Fost and..."

"And what?" demanded Hylak.

"I heard the humans have taken all the cells they could locate. We have barely enough for you to get to Earth."

* * *

All strike teams checked in and were returning to the control center. As they came into the area, some with prisoners—all with collected weapons, they were divided into two groups. One group guarded the captured soldiers and civilians and the other was put to work loading the shoms with the injured, the dead and all the energy cells and weapons they could find.

Darce landed near the control center and ordered the prisoners to be taken to join their fellows. Carsteen approached with a large group of humans, "Well, Captain Gannon, it seems as though we have a small victory."

"So far, so good," returned Darce, "but we still have a long way to go."

Team leaders gathered close, and Darce raised his voice, "We're far from done ladies and gentlemen. Our next task is loading the shoms and getting up to the space station."

Jason reminded Darce, "Order of importance...division of labor."

"Right," said Darce. "First, we need to secure the prisoners with ten armed guards."

Connor Brinkman came forward, "I'll take twenty men with me and secure the prisoners then with the available extras, we'll sweep the island looking for others we've missed and collect any weapons and energy cells we find."

Jason said, "I'll organize the dead and wounded onto the first shom along with all medical personnel. They'll be in the first group to go up to the station."

Tetra loaded the Blue Wolf with another twenty people and six large energy cells, "I'll get the Wolf ready for its task when everyone is aboard."

Carsteen supervised getting the other available shoms loaded with people and energy cells. Each shom was maxed out load-wise and the succession of vessels flying up to the station, offloading and returning to the surface began. Each round-trip took three hours and the work went on for over twelve hours.

The final count was 1,712 live healthy humans, 23 injured and 12 dead. The fuel, food and water that had been gathered at the Cube, was loaded and the last two shoms lifted off to the station. Upon arrival, these shoms were secured with their cargo still on board. Storgon was taken to the bridge where he was secured to a tilted panel and placed under armed guard.

Jason and Connor Brinkman made the last trip to the energy collector where they placed several large energy cells at critical locations. Finally, back aboard the Mulbor Kray, Frank Linsman coordinated the disconnect from the space station and gradually moved the transport vessel away from the two large structures.

Darce, Tetra and Jason boarded the Blue Wolf, left the Mulbor and began their targeting run at the collection facility.

2246.04.03.09.46 (Off-World) Aboard the Blue Wolf

"The Mulbor is now at a safe distance," said Tetra, "we can proceed."

Jason scanned the facility and targeted the several locations where they had placed the large energy cylinders, "Targets locked in and ready, fire when ready."

"We're at a distance of six kilometers," said Darce. He opened his com-link to Frank Linsman, "Preparing to fire on the target."

Frank returned with, "Copy that."

Darce looked at Tetra and Jason, "Are you ready for some fireworks?"

Jason nodded and Tetra scanned her instruments one more time, "As ever was, Captain," she returned, "you may fire when ready," she added with a smile.

"Mulbor Kray this is the Blue Wolf," Darce spoke into his com-link. "We are ready to launch missiles into the structures, please stand by."

"Blue Wolf, this is Mulbor Kray," said Frank Linsman. "We are approaching fifty kilometers from the target. We are clear and ready to accept you back aboard when your mission is complete."

"Copy that," said Darce. "Firing in three, two, one..."

The missiles were aimed at the three points of connection between the two structures where Jason and Connor had placed the energy cells. "Impact in three, two, one...," said Tetra.

As the missiles flew toward their targets, the Blue Wolf accelerated toward the rendezvous with the Mulbor. The missiles struck their targets within a second of each other and the initial explosion tore the two structures apart, then within another second the secondary explosions of the energy cells engulfed the entire assembly in a ball of fire. The shock wave reached the Blue Wolf, rocking the craft, but doing no significant damage.

"That was closer than I figured," said Jason.

The three breathed a sigh of relief as they checked the Wolf's systems and began to relax in their seats.

"All systems good," said Tetra. "I've got the Mulbor on scanner—rendezvous in twenty-three minutes."

The calm was interrupted by Frank Linsman, "Darce, we have company."

"I'm getting something coming on the scanners," said Tetra.

"Can you define it?" asked Darce.

"Uh, oh," said Tetra, "I'm getting multiple readings...four, five, six smaller and one larger."

"Like the Karnis Tarb and its six little Cains?" speculated Darce.

"Or it's identical twin," said Jason. "I'll reload the missile tubes, ready in five minutes."

"Make it quicker if you can," said Darce. "Mulbor, we will be slightly delayed in returning to you. Move away as much as you can—if this doesn't work, you may have to leave without us."

Jason contacted Connor Brinkman, "Time to man the side firing ports, we may be in a contest to get outta here."

2246.04.03.11.33 (Off-World)   Aboard the Mulbor Kray

"I'll take the port side," said Connor as he tapped several other men and led them to the weapon cache. "Take four tubes each and be sure you have the right armbands."

The Mulbor had now reached a separation distance of fifty-eight kilometers, "Speed now .15LS-4," said Linsman. "Increase speed to .25LS-4."

"Do we have a fix on the Tarb?" asked Connor.

A technician responded, "The Enkar Tarb as indicated on the scanner panel, I have him locked in, sir."

"Direct the main cannon at the Enkar Tarb," said Connor "and hold."

2246.04.03.12.53 (Off-World) Aboard the Blue Wolf

Jason yelled at Darce, "Tubes loaded and primed, give me coordinates and we'll swat some of these flies."

Darce took the Blue Wolf in a wide arc, moving farther away from the Mulbor, "Are you two ready?"

"Give me some numbers Cap," said Tetra.

Darce spat out the first set of coordinates and Tetra entered the info into the targeting computer, "Fire when ready Cap."

The first missile exited the firing tube and began its own arc, chasing the targeted Cain. The impact was a huge ball of fire, and the Cain was obliterated. Tetra had moved to the co-pilot's seat and entered the next set of coordinates. Again, the missile resulted in complete destruction of the second Cain.

As Darce zigged and zagged and finally dropped several hundred meters, the Dar'Wannian Cains fired four times at the Wolf and only hit the outer edge of the starboard wing, causing very little damage.

Tetra had targeted three Cains and was trying to find a fourth when Darce said, "I think he has a lock on us, fire what you have...now!"

Tetra launched three missiles and immediately returned to finding the other Cain. The three missiles all locked and impacted within two seconds. Total, four Cains down and two to go plus the Enkar Tarb.

2246.04.03.13.27 (Off-world) Aboard the Mulbor Kray

"Darce," said Linsman, "we are prepared to fire at the Enkar. Please stand by."

The large cannon was fully energized, and the discharge of energy formed a perfectly straight line from the Mulbor Kray over a hundred kilometers away to the Tarb. The silent blast of energy through the void struck its target and tore a hole through the Enkar Tarb's main engine compartment. The Tarb lost all control and began to come apart, scattering pieces of the vessel and its occupants in space.

2246.04.03.13.34 (Off-World) Aboard the Blue Wolf

"Darce, I have the last of the Cains locked in," said Tetra.

The Cain began to maneuver into position to fire its cannon at the Blue Wolf and Darce yelled, "Take him out!"

Tetra launched the missile and Darce set coordinates for the Mulbor, moving in a zig-zag pattern to avoid an energy blast from the pursuing Cain. As the missile struck the Cain, the Blue Wolf was accelerating toward the transport vessel. "Time to get outta this neighborhood," said Darce looking at Tetra.

*　　*　　*

SEVENTEEN

2246.04.03.21.14 (Off-World) Wan'Markan, Dar'Wan

A signal was sent to Dar'Wan from the control center on Dar'Fost as the attacks by the humans began. Flamnar ordered all their remaining vessels at Dar'Wan and those in their galaxy be placed on high-alert status and prime attention directed at recapturing the escaping humans. The taking of the Mulbor Kray was totally unexpected, as was the plan to escape to Earth.

"Can these humans operate our vessels, the Kray, the Tarbs, our shuttles and cargo vessels?" asked Flamnar.

"We tried to learn as much as we could about their military capabilities," said Marshall. "The talk of new weapons which we are only now hearing about led us to open too many doors to them. In retrospect, they have been very observant, watching as we operated the Kray and the cargo units. They obviously learn very quickly."

"Is it possible for them to reach Earth?" questioned Flamnar. "Can they operate the hyperdrive?"

"The humans were assumed to be less than capable of taking control of the Mulbor," returned Marshall, "and thus such a scenario was never considered." He thought for a moment and continued, "If they don't use the hyperdrive," he speculated, "they would remain at sub-light velocities and die before they left our system."

As the two were speaking, Marshall received another communication. "The new collection facility—they have fired on it...it has been destroyed." He looked confused and panicked. "The concentration and storage unit has also been destroyed." He listened to more of the communication from Dar'Fost. "Apparently the humans have taken all the energy cylinders from Dar'Fost, leaving us with only the supply we have here and whatever we can gather in this original collection center."

"Production here is not enough to sustain the planet much less pursue the humans across the galaxy," said Flamnar. "How many of the large cylinders do we have?"

"A few," responded Marshall. "The Enkar is fully fueled, has two large cylinders and five smaller ones and may be at Dar'Fost now."

"Can the Enkar stop the Mulbor," asked Flamnar.

"If the humans have taken the Mulbor and moved far enough away, we may not be able to stop it in flight," said Marshall. "We'd have to wait for it to arrive at Earth and retake it there along with the extra cylinders."

"Yes, I see. Send the Karnis to Earth as soon as it is finished refueling to await them," said Flamnar. "Then when the Borstor is ready, we may know better where it will be needed."

Marshall relayed the orders and said, "What else can we do?"

"What else could we have done?" said Flamnar, "We should have waited until we had completed the replacement of this older center." He paced back and forth, thinking.

"There is no choice, we need those cylinders and the Mulbor Kray. Marshall, assemble the war council, we need all the input we can get, and we must act quickly, or we will have lost the Earth as a new home."

Two of the Tarb class vessels, the Karnis the Enkar, along with their complement of six Cains each were committed. The Enkar was assumed to be at Dar'Fost although several attempts to make contact had failed and the Karnis, in the middle of refueling and several minor repairs was put on a rush status. The Borster was still headed to Dar'Wan and would be in need of similar refueling when it arrived.

2246.04.03.23.28 (Off-World) Aboard the Blue Wolf

The Blue Wolf gained speed as it crossed the void of space between the space station and the Mulbor Kray. Darce hailed the transport, "Mulbor Kray, we are leaving orbit about Dar'Fost and heading to the rendezvous point."

"Copy that," returned Frank Linsman, "we have you on scanners and will send a flight path for meeting and boarding."

"Mulbor, this is Blue Wolf," said Darce into his com-link. "I have you on visual, approaching on assigned path and matching speed. Request permission to come aboard."

Frank responded, "Blue Wolf, all systems green for entry in cargo bay."

Darce brought the Blue Wolf alongside of the Mulbor, slowly moved inside the door and set down on the closest circle.

The cargo bay doors closed, and the atmosphere was reintroduced into the area. Frank tapped his com-link, "Welcome aboard folks, the atmosphere is now safe in the bay."

Darce looked at his companions and said, "Major, Sergeant, shall we debark?"

"After you, Captain," returned Tetra.

"After you, Major," said Darce. As Tetra stepped out, Darce looked at Jason, "Shall we?"

"Aye Captain," returned Jason as they stepped off together.

2246.04.04.02.16 (Off-world) Aboard the Mulbor Kray

Frank Linsman ordered the Blue Wolf be secured in the cargo bay, then requested Darce join him on the bridge. The Mulbor began to move slowly away from the Korta system and out of the Perdone Galaxy, toward the Milky Way and home. As Darce entered the bridge, the entire four bridge crews crowded the area and Darce went to the commander's station. Frank was about to step aside for Darce, but Darce held up a hand, this one's by you, Frank. Let's see what this baby can do."

"I'd suggest we gradually increase speed until we hit the LS+4 level, Darce," said Linsman.

"You're driving, Frank. Carry on."

The Mulbor's systems responded to the control commands the crew input. When the hyperdrive system was activated, the main view- screen showed the space in front of the vessel and projected several parabolic curves extending out into space. "Systems online," said Linsman, "navigation, do we have anchor points selected?"

A tech standing at a control panel responded, "Aye sir, four points selected."

"Energize anchors and set speed at factor one," said Linsman. "This is our first time around, Helm, so bring her up slowly."

"Aye, sir," returned the Helm.

Immediately several dashed, grey lines appeared on screen and gradually turned red as the vessel inside the extending energy shield remained at a constant speed. The shield extended farther into space and accelerated. The vessel began to show alien characters on screen, probably advising of speed and position among other things. Additional dashed, grey lines appeared on the screen.

Frank glanced at Storgon as he remained secured to his padded panel, "How am I doing so far, Commander?"

Storgon nodded, "Actually, well done for your first time, Mister Linsman."

Carsteen looked at Storgon, "You may call him Captain, Commander."

Storgon acknowledged the title, looked at Frank and said firmly, "Captain Linsman."

Carsteen then turned to Frank and said, "You're officially promoted."

* * *

The Space Station above Dar'Fost was destroyed along with the adjoining energy collection and concentration facility and the Mulbor Kray was accelerating toward home. The humans had taken as many energy cylinders as they could find on the planet's surface and left only three craft capable of flight. None of the Dar'Wannian vessels were capable of reaching the home planet and they were ordered to conserve all sources of energy they could find.

2246.04.04.07.33 (Off-World) Wan'Markan, Dar'Wan

Flamnar and Marshall met their war council where the possibility of the Enkar being disabled or destroyed was considered.

"It would have taken a direct hit by one of our main energy cannons at mid or high power," said one of the Commanders. "Are the humans able to operate the weapons system?"

"We don't know what they have learned or deduced," said Marshall, "we must assume they are fully capable of the vessel's full complement of weapons and drive options."

After much discussion and debate it was determined the best action was to send the Karnis to Earth in hopes of arriving ahead of the Mulbor and the Borstor to Dar'Fost to be refueled. "The Borstor will collect as much stored energy as they can find and immediately leave for Earth," said Flamnar.

"Agreed," said Marshall. "They can also determine the status of the Enkar."

"Yes," said Flamnar, "but do not delay their departure to Earth with the resupply of cylinders."

* * *

2246.04.04.09.46 (Off-World) Aboard the Karnis Tarb

"We are about to energize the hyperdrive and expect to arrive before the Mulbor Kray. Our next communication will be when we return, hopefully very soon."

Flamnar received the message and responded, "Yes, remember, do not destroy the Mulbar, we will be needing it."

Hylak immediately ordered energy evaluations and weapons verifications. "We must be prepared to engage the Mulbar as well as the Earthlings fighter craft, their *tach birds.*"

"An advantage may lie in their inability to use the travel in hyperspace as effectively as we do. Hopefully you will be able to reach their solar system before them and eliminate any assistance they may gain from their forces. What is the higher limit of your drive on the Karnis Tarb?"

"If we use more of the concentrated energy to accelerate directly through space from here to Earth, rather than using the several legs as in our last trip, we will be able to save some time," said Hylak, "perhaps more than the advantage they have already realized."

"Make it so Commander and advise us when you are prepared to enter Hyperspace," said Flamnar.

Hylak restated his orders for evaluations and his crew responded, "Almost done," came a reply. "We are replacing a fuel cell for the drive systems and have replaced one of the weapon energy cells," replied an aide. "Work will be done very soon." The aide responded to a communication on his com-link and contacted Hylak again, "Sir, Commander Storgon has been taken prisoner aboard the Mulbor."

Flamnar was silent for a moment then, "Excellent. Storgon is a very capable commander and should realize the importance of our retaking the Mulbor. He would also know they must arrive at its destination with all systems operable. He knows we will not fire upon the Mulbor. He is very safe."

"We may begin our voyage within the next hour," said Hylak. "We have requested any available energy cells we may use. Our current supply would allow travel to and from Earth, but we'd spend almost all available energy in combat with Earth's tach birds and without resupply, we may not be able to return."

"The Kansat Kray and the Borstor Tarb have been recalled to Dar'Wan to be refit and made ready for travel in hyperspace. They will follow you to Earth as soon as possible with a resupply of energy cells and a complement of Cains," said Flamnar.

"Food and water as well?" asked Hylak.

"Yes, of course," returned Flamnar, "but understand, we must retake the Mulbar. It is absolutely critical in the conquering of Earth."

The Karnis Tarb was finally ready, "All systems ready, flight path resolved, and we are ready to engage systems," said Hylak.

"We will follow as soon as possible," said Flamnar.

* * *

2246.04.04.11.27 (Off-World) Aboard the Mulbor Kray

Carsteen leaned against a backboard on the bridge, watching the activity of the control crew, "How are we doing, Darce?" he asked.

"We've locked on to Sagittarius A Star and we're moving at a speed we've never seen before and the images coming in through the view screen don't help much. Understand, what we see in the view of Sagittarius A is about thirty-thousand years old, and the view of our arm of the Milky Way was generated fifteen to twenty years ago. So, we're being pulled toward Sagittarius which will get us close to our solar system. Our plan is to break the anchor to Sagittarius and decrease speed when we think we have covered about half the distance to Earth, have a good look at our position and recalculate our next step, probably picking a new anchor star and continue another half the remaining distance. All this starting and stopping will use up a lot of energy and we'll probably use twice the energy necessary by the trip's end. This is all new to all of us."

"And we're on our own out here," added Tetra as she looked at Storgon.

Darce turned to Storgon, "Our friend knows all too well we must arrive intact for both sides. They need this vessel to continue the conquest of Earth and we need it to get home. First, we arrive in our neighborhood and then we will probably encounter the Karnis Tarb and its little Cains."

"As soon as we can, Earth must be made aware of the impending attack," said Carsteen.

"We can't communicate with Earth yet," said Jason, "any communication sent from here will take years to reach our solar system. When we reach the outer limits of the Kuiper, we'll send a message and open a dialogue with Earth and our space stations."

"You're sure they'll come after us," asked Carsteen. "We've destroyed their energy collection capability. Maybe they'll figure we smashed into a star, an asteroid, or another planet—and we're just so much space debris."

"Wishful thinking," returned Darce. "They have one other transport vessel, the Kansat. It's about half the Mulbor's size and capability and was in repairs when we left."

"Extensive repairs," added Jason, "and from what I gathered, the energy needed to run their planet will use up every ounce of capability of their remaining collection facility leaving nothing for the Kansat to travel to Earth."

"It may be wishful thinking," added Tetra, "but we can't afford a chance. I say we figure they are already on their way to Earth and maybe even able to arrive before us."

Carsteen looked puzzled, "In what, that Karnis Vessel?"

"Most likely, yes, the Karnis," said Darce. "Complete with its six Cains, ready to take us on."

"This is a huge target and not that maneuverable," said Carsteen, "we may have traveled a long way just to get blown away at the finish line."

"I don't think so," said Darce, "they need this vessel. They don't want to destroy it or even cripple it. They need it intact and fully functional."

* * *

2246.04.04.16.14 (Off-world) Aboard the Karnis Tarb

"Commander, do they have a flight path?" asked Bynton, Hylak's second-in-command.

"I don't see how they could have, but we must assume they do," replied Hylak. "And remember, Storgon is aboard. He will assist them in reaching their planet where we can catch them."

"Energy, do they have enough energy cells, and do they know how to change them out during flight?"

"I assume they either know how to make the changes or Storgon would advise them," said Hylak.

"Yes," returned Bynton, "if Storgon is allowed to speak."

"I would think these humans would realize the implications of losing their energy source at the speed at which they travel," said Hylak. "Perhaps they would slow to a sub-hyperdrive speed to make the changes."

"If they don't?"

"If they lose the energy field in front of them at hyper-speed," said Hylak, "the vessel would disintegrate."

Bynton thought for a moment, then asked, "How did they learn to control the Mulbor?"

"We made a few mistakes in treating the humans," said Hylak. "First, we assumed they would accept their position as residents of Dar'Fost. They could have had several generations before the collisions occurred. Second, we gave them more freedom than we should have in an attempt to gain more information about their weapons systems."

"They learned to fly our shoms, but not the Kray," said Bynton.

"Yes," said Hylak "and they observed everything we did on board each vessel."

"Clever little creatures, these humans," said Bynton. "Yes, they are."

*   *   *

2246.04.04.17.05 (Off-World) Aboard the Mulbor Kray

Jason checked the starfield in front of them, the total energy consumed, the time lapsed on board and tapped his com-link, "Darce, we're ready to make our first stop and re-evaluate our flight."

"Copy that," returned Darce. He looked at Storgon, "We're going to drop out of hyperspace for an evaluation of our position and systems check. Do you have any advice at this point, or will you allow us to stumble on our own?"

"You think I will assist you?" quizzed Storgon. "I should probably allow you to make a mistake and watch as we are crushed and scattered as so much dust."

"You know it's in both our interests to successfully reach our solar system," said Carsteen. "I assume your friends are on their way there to meet us and reclaim this vessel."

"Yes, Mr. President," said Storgon, "you are correct. I will advise you on the changing of energy cells." He looked at Darce, "Captain, please adjust your speed factor lower, the third notch on the controller, then wait a moment before the second reduction."

"Is it necessary to be at a complete stop when we change the energy cells?" asked Jason.

"No, not a complete stop, but something below your LS-4 level," said Storgon. "The lower the speed, the better."

Darce began the reduction in speed and the image on the view screen clarified. The star field was no longer streaks of light, but points of light that still flew past.

Jason and Tetra both looked for an identifiable system or group of stars, "I'm not getting much yet, but I do see the sector of our system," said Jason. "We can anchor to another star from here and move closer."

Tetra agreed, "I see several candidates, one may even be our sun."

Darce adjusted the speed control again and the vessel slowed to an acceptable level approximately equal to LS-5. He looked at Storgon, "Slow enough?"

"Yes," returned the alien. "now you may begin the changing of fuel cells."

* * *

2246.04.04.19.41 (Off-World) Aboard the Karnis Tarb

Bynton paced nervously near Hylak's console, "I believe they should be making a fuel cell change very soon."

"Yes, and this is where we may pass them," said Hylak, "or we could slow to a communication speed and see if we can find them."

"Slow?" returned Bynton, "Why would they slow, do you think they don't know how to change fuel cells while in hyperspace?"

"I don't know and I'm sure Storgon would not show them that process. So, let's assume they have slowed and are in the process of changing the drive engine's fuel cell."

"If we can find them, verify they are changing cells, we'll be able to get to earth before them."

"They will see us as easily as we see them."

"Yes," said Hylak, "but at the same time, we let Storgon know we are near."

* * *

2246.04.04.22.09 (Off-World) Aboard the Mulbor Kray

The Mulbor slowed to a sub LS-4 speed and the work began on changing the fuel cell. Storgon was present, directing some of the movements, "Be sure the discharge is fully closed before disconnecting the fuel cell. We do not want a discharge of any residual energy escaping into this vessel."

Jason and Tetra both watched very closely as the work proceeded. When completed, they went into an empty room and listed the numerous steps employed, writing down everything they noticed. "Seems like a few extra steps in this sequence," said Jason.

"I noticed the same thing," said Tetra. "He's probably trying to give his friends as much time as possible to catch up and even get ahead of us."

"I suspect these few steps were unnecessary," said Jason, pointing to several items on their list, "but I'm not positive."

"Best we follow the same procedure if we need to change it again," said Tetra.

The change was complete and Darce ordered everybody back to their stations and the start sequence for the hyper-drive system was initiated. "Back on track, Mr. President," said Darce. "Do we have a new heading, Jason?"

"Aye Captain," returned Jason. "On our heading come to bearing 17.5 mark 0."

The vessel was redirected, and Jason continued, "On course, Captain. You may energize the drive system."

The Mulbor began to accelerate slowly and soon the energy field with the vessel was moving toward the solar system and Earth through hyperspace at near LS+4.

"We should be in our old neighborhood in less than three days," said Jason.

* * *

2246.04.05.04.03 (Off-World) Aboard the Karnis Tarb

"We have sent out a hailing several times, Commander," said Bynton. "There have been no returns."

"Understood. The message may not have reached them, or they have not stopped yet. It all depends on the speed at which they travel and how soon the energy will be used. We will now resume our travel, only now at a greater speed. Prepare the crew to begin the acceleration."

"Yes sir," responded Bynton with a worried look on his face.

* * *

2246.04.05.09.45 (Off-World) Aboard the Mulbor Kray

"All systems in order," said Darce from the command position. "Let's be absolutely sure, run the checklist every hour."

"Copy that," returned Jason as he checked his link.

The Mulbor seemed to be standing still as the total energy field moved through space toward their destination. At the first of the hourly checks, "All systems here green," reported Tetra.

"Same here," reported Jason. Almost immediately, an alarm sounded, and a light began to flash above the main viewing screen, "Darce, something is happening."

Darce studied the control panel in front of him and looked puzzled. Storgon became fully alert and shouted, "I must see the control panel...NOW!"

Darce signaled one of the guards watching Storgon and he was released. He came immediately to Darce's panel, looked at the controls and made an adjustment to the main view screen. The image on the screen changed to a series of spinning parabolic curves in three dimensions and as many colors. Another few control moves and the screen showed a red netlike curve with a small dent near the apex. "We approach an object," said Storgon. "Perhaps an asteroid, maybe a planet. We must set an anchor and avoid this one." He positioned himself in front of the control panel and moved several dials and switches. The view screen showed a straight white line from the bottom center of the screen to the dent in the red net. A few more control moves and the white line moved to a point that pleased Storgon. "There," he said in a relaxed tone. "We will move around this one and have to adjust again once it has been passed."

"Would we have collided with that object?" asked Darce, looking at Storgon.

"Probably not," returned Storgon, "but it could have taken us off course and required further adjustments."

"Thank you," said Carsteen.

"I did not do this for you, Mr. President, it is critical we arrive fully intact."

Darce, Jason and Tetra huddled away from the bridge, "Did you follow the movements at the panel?" asked Darce.

Both replied in the negative, "I caught a few toward the end of his action," said Jason, "but I completely missed the first several inputs."

"Same here," said Tetra, "what about you, Darce?"

"Totally took me by surprise," said Darce. "I saw a few things, but he was in my way. We should try to write down everything he did, including the blanks in our minds. If this happens again, we can catch more—maybe."

* * *

2246.04.05.11.06 (Off-world) Aboard the Mulbor Kray

Bynton approached Hylak, "Sir, we've received a distress signal from the Mulbor."

"Verbal?"

"No sir, the automatic signal, sent three times in succession." Hylak nodded, "Good, Storgon has let us know all is well."

* * *

2246.04.05.14.08 (Off-world) Aboard the Mulbor Kray

"We have passed the obstacle," said Storgon, "now we must readjust our course."

Darce looked at the view screen, "What am I seeing on the screen, Storgon?"

"The blue lines are the forcefield in front of us, the obstacle in our path is in red, and the anchor was initially white," said Storgon. "The anchor was in the negative forcing the two apart and causing the white to turn yellow as it continues to increase the distance between the two. It is no longer needed; we can cancel it and verify our next anchor."

"Where is our anchor to Sagittarius?" asked Jason.

Storgon stood at the control panel again and changed the view screen bringing up a white line to a star in the Milky Way. "There is your primary anchor line," he replied. "And now to delete the yellow anchor," he said as he made a few movements at the panel.

Tetra noticed a series of symbols scrolling across the screen as they talked, "I assume these are speed, fuel and directional readings.

"Yes," said Storgon. "Our fuel supply is near full, range at current speed is well outside your planet's orbit and our speed is at factor three."

"So, we'll have to change out the fuel cell at least once more," speculated Jason.

"Yes," returned Storgon.

Darce remained at his control station for another hour, watching the view screen and the changing lines. A periodic signal would indicate additional dashed grey lines to various objects and Storgon finally gave in, "Yes, captain, you may connect secondary anchors if you wish. They may allow a greater speed or simply a more economic use of the energy." He approached the control panel, "If I may," as he touched a symbol on the panel several more white lines formed to another object. "This will reduce the demand on the prime anchor and use less energy in total maintaining the same speed."

Darce nodded and had watched as closely as he could, "When another potential line appears, would I have to accept or reject it?"

"Neither," said Storgon, "inaction at the control will result in no action. Understand these potential anchors are not always advantageous. Some could actually result in damage to the vessel."

"So, I shouldn't try to make adjustments based on little grey lines?"

"I would not recommend such, Captain, but I will be here, and we could discuss any such occurrences."

As they were talking Frank Linsman approached, "Captain, are you ready for a break?"

Darce looked around the bridge, saw the next crew was taking over individual stations and he turned to Linsman, "It's all yours Captain Linsman." He looked at Jason and said, "I'm hungry, you ready for some grub?"

"Sounds like a plan," said Jason.

"May I join you two?" asked Tetra.

"Our pleasure, Major," replied Jason. The three left the Bridge, found Jacob Carsteen, "Mr. President, please join us for dinner, or is it lunch?"

Tetra laughed, "I guess time of day doesn't mean much out here zipping through the cosmos at some ridiculous multiple of light-speed."

They sat together with their food and discussed the current situation, "I'm comfortable with Storgon assisting on the bridge," said Darce. "It's very much in their advantage for us to reach our system."

"My feelings exactly," said Carsteen. "I am troubled by his touching the control panel—as if he was sending a message to his comrades, although I have no idea what he may have told them."

"What's to tell," said Jason. "Our location or our time of arrival? There's no mystery there. I would guess he wants to let them know he is with us, and we will make it to near Earth."

"So, what's our plan?" asked Tetra. "We have to get to a station that can accept the prisoners they took, then they'll want their Mulbor back."

"Why not enter the SW Earth orbit on the other side of the system, away from SW-27, perhaps at SW-26," suggested Jason. "We off-load our passengers and all the energy cells, then take the Mulbor out beyond the Kuiper and blow it up."

"And how do we get back home?" asked Darce.

"The Blue Wolf," said Tetra. "They have given us more than enough of the smaller energy cells for us to make it back."

"So, how many Tarbs and Cains are there for us to contend with?" asked Carsteen.

"A good question," returned Darce. "There was at least one Tarb at SW-13 and it probably had six Cains."

"Yes, the Borstor Tarb," said Tetra, "I asked Frank Linsman, but he didn't know if it stayed there, or returned to Dar'Wan."

"Let's figure the worst," said Darce, "assume the Borstor is still in our system. So, we'll have two Tarbs and probably twelve Cains to deal with."

"Before we destroy the Mulbor, we could use it to get close to the bogy's vessels," suggested Jason. "Then, surprise!"

"Yeah, surprise alright when they have us outnumbered fourteen to one," said Darce.

"We also have about thirty of their little boom sticks and the armbands. I have an outdoor suit, an EMU, in a storage locker," said Tetra.

Jason shook his head, "Have you worn the suit, Major?"

"No, but I'm sure it will work," said Tetra.

Jason continued to shake his head, "Tetra, it's what I do, the suit, if it fits me, I'll do the outside walk. Those suits are difficult to maneuver in if you're not familiar with them. You and Darce have the Wolf and you have ten very sharp teeth on board."

"I have to agree with him," said Darce, "Jason has wrestled many of the objects we collected while cleaning up the space around Earth. And he's good at it."

"I'll go check the suit now," said Jason as he looked at Tetra. "Locker eleven," she said. "Good luck."

* * *

2246.04.05.17.35 (Off-World) Aboard the Karnis Tarb

"As soon as we drop out of Hyperspace," said Hylak, "try to contact the Borstor and verify their location and status. They don't yet know what is happening. Then verify our fuel supply, the energy cells may be near depletion."

Bynton nodded and said, "The Enkar—we received a message stating it was destroyed at Dar'Fost along with the planet's space station and the collection facility."

* * *

Both vessels, the Mulbor and the Karnis, were moving through space in near parallel paths. Neither could see the other nor knew where they were. On board the Karnis Tarb, it was known that the Mulbor had reached an approximate position less than halfway to Earth. The signal sent by Storgon told them very little, but they did know the Mulbor had slowed for a cell change and encountered an obstacle. The Karnis also encountered an obstacle and Hylak wondered if it was the same one.

2246.04.05.23.27 (Off-World) Aboard the Mulbor Kray

The journey was now in its fourth day by Carsteen's calculations, "Are we getting close?" he asked.

"Approaching the Oort Cloud now," said Darce. "We'll slow to the LS+3 level and should be through in about fourteen hours. Then it's about another eight or nine hours to the Kuiper, and as many to navigate through that mess, and a few more to home?

"Two more days?" said Carsteen.

"Sounds right," returned Darce. "So, we'd best get ourselves ready for an encounter or two."

"We've collected as many of the Dar'Wannian tube weapons as we could find," said Jason. "We're now matching up the armbands and checking the energy levels. We'll have about fifty ready to use very soon."

2246.04.06.03.17 (Off-World) Aboard the Karnis Tarb

Hylak had navigated the Oort and Kuiper before and based on that experience and the much smaller craft he piloted; knew he could move through both in much less time than the Mulbor. He also depended on Storgon slowing the humans progress as much as possible, giving him time to assume a position near SW-27 before the arrival of the Mulbor.

* * *

EIGHTEEN

2246.04.06.03.17 (Off-World) Aboard the Karnis Tarb

The Karnis Tarb made its way through the outer asteroid belts and assumed a position in weapons range of SW-27. "Report from the Borstor," said Bynton. "They're finishing an inspection of the several SW stations in the Earth's orbit, including the Lunar ones. They'll be close by in four Earth hours."

"Good," said Hylak. "Have them assume a position opposite SW-27 at the same distance we've assumed."

"Anything else?" asked Bynton.

"Yes," returned Hylak. "He should prepare all his Cains for close battle with the Earthling fighters, but caution him, do not damage the Mulbor. We need it to get back to Dar'Wan."

"I believe the humans only have the one vessel to fight us;" stated Bynton, "their Blue Wolf."

"They were able to pilot the Mulbor across a great distance, they undoubtedly have the ability to pilot the Cains as well."

"How many Cains could they have?"

"I don't know," said Hylak, "I don't know."

2246.04.06.03.46 (Off-World) Aboard the Mulbor Kray

"Approaching SW-26, Captain," said a tech.

"Jason, take the president, Storgon, and all the injured aboard the Blue Wolf and get them aboard SW-26. If they have any tach birds available, we can bring them aboard and get closer to the Cains and Tarbs before we engage."

"Copy that," said Jason. "Let me know when it's safe to make the transfer." He left the bridge, found Dr. Morrison, and began loading the injured aboard the Blue Wolf. The transfer of injured and medical personnel went off without a hitch. Then came the moving of other personnel off of the Mulbor Kray.

2246.04.06.04.07 (Off-World) Aboard the Karnis Tarb

"We're getting sensor readings from Station SW-26," reported Bynton. "It seems as though the humans are off-loading their passengers there. Should we attack them?"

"No," replied Hylak, "if there are no humans left on the Mulbor, it will be less desirable for them to hold on to it."

"What then?"

"Then perhaps we could negotiate the return of our transport vessel," said Hylak.

2246.04.06.05.28 (Off-World) Aboard the Mulbor Kray

"Darce, we're not getting a reaction from the Karnis or the Borstor," said Tetra, "they must be aware we are offloading our people."

Connor Brinkman approached, "They want this vessel, and they want it intact. So, our unloading it works for them." He paused, looking about the emptying vessel and continued, "Negotiate, it's a possibility they would try to negotiate the return of this beast even if it's damaged in the process, it may still be of great value to them."

"Damaged?" quizzed Jason.

"If the damage were restricted to those non-vital parts, parts that could be repaired either before or after a return trip to Dar'Wan."

"Like the cargo bay and not the bridge?" suggested Tetra.

"Exactly, they put a few holes in the vessel walls, and we'd want out...they could retrieve their prize and run."

"So, how many tach birds do we have?" asked Darce.

"This station still has four birds fully charged and ready to fly," said a familiar voice.

"Colonel Hansby," said Darce, "what are you doing up here?"

"Getting ready for just this sort of thing. We've done a great deal of thinking and planning for this. As soon as we knew you were on your way here, we started to pull things together."

"What else is in the works?" asked Darce.

"We're calling in all available tach birds, topping off their batteries and giving them a full complement of weapons."

"Nukes?" asked Jason.

"Not all," returned Hansby. "Each bird is carrying two old nukes along with their usual laser cannons and a dozen conventional missiles."

"Maybe we can add to that arsenal," said Jason as he handed Hansby an energy tube. "This little thing at three quarter power can take down one of the aliens' Cains. Set the energy blast at full and you may get three or four blasts out of it. Set it lower and you get more blasts, but less powerful."

"What do we do with them?" asked Hansby.

"You'd have to be outside the tach bird. They fire a blast of negative energy when the operator squeezes the tube," replied Jason. "The armband has to be less than a half-meter away and around the operator's forearm. So, the way to use them would be to put the armband on, preset at about 75% power and the spacesuit over that. The operator holds the tube. He points it at a target and when he squeezes it, the blast comes out like a laser."

"So, our guy is outside, that's risky as hell," said Hansby.

"Takes a special kind of guy," said Tetra.

Jason walked over to one of the tach birds, "We button up the bridge, open the top loading hatch, stand on a low platform and secure the man and suit, so he can't get more of himself outta the bird. Then fire off as many blasts as he can and pull himself back inside and secure the hatch."

Darce looked at Jason, "Yeah, then what'll ya do?"

"Recharge and go back out."

"I don't like it," said Darce.

"Neither do I," said Jason, "but it'll work."

2246.04.06.06.22 (Off-World) Aboard the Mulbor Kray

"What is our energy status?" asked Hylak.

"About ten percent of total," returned Blynton, "not enough to use the large weapon and be able to navigate."

"The Cains?" asked Hylak.

"They are all fully charged," returned Blynton, "but that is what drained our main power."

"Check with the Borstor," ordered Hylak, "one of us should be able to return home."

2246.04.06.06.29 (Off-World) Aboard the Borstor Tarb

"Commander, a message from the Karnis," said a tech on board the Borstor.

"Good," replied Sajten Nostog. "Check our energy levels here and on each of the Cains."

The tech returned within several minutes, "We are at fifteen-percent and each of the Cain's supply is about half."

"Let Commander Hylak know our situation, send it in our language, in case anyone else is listening."

2246.04.06.10.12 (Off-World) Aboard the Mulbor Kray

"Modifications have been made to all the tach birds," said Hansby. "They all now have an energy tube capability through the top hatch and all the crews have been shown how they work. We're ready to engage."

"Sir, we intercepted a message from the Borstor," said one of the techs.

"What does it say?" asked Darce.

"It's in their language. You could ask our guest," said the tech looking at Storgon.

Darce thought for a moment, "No, better not."

* * *

The tach birds were loaded on the Mulbor Kray, and the crews stood ready. The tubes were fully charged, the men were dressed in their spacesuits and anchor straps were all in place. Darce found Tetra, "Hey, I'm gonna take the Blue Wolf with Jason and do a little damage to those Cains and Tarbs. You stay with Frank and when the battle heats up, you guys get outta the area. They most likely won't want fire on the Mulbor, but let's not take any chances."

Tetra looked Darce in the eye, "I'd really like you to come back Darce."

They stared at each other for a minute and Darce finally said, "Yeah, I'll be back."

* * *

The Mulbor Kray pulled away from SW-26 and began its trip to the other side of the Earth and SW-27. The crew consisted of fourteen tach birds modified with energy tube capability and two older nukes each, along with their standard laser cannons.

The Mulbor's sensors indicated the presence of two Tarb class vessels along with their standard six Cains each. As they approached, the Cains began to detach from the Tarbs and move into attack formations. The Karnis hailed the Mulbor and the Mulbor responded, "This is Frank Linsman. I am in control of the Mulbor Kray, what are your intentions?"

Hylak responded, "You have taken our transport vessel and we want it back."

"We hesitate to give you this vessel if you will only return to Earth again and continue your attempted conquest. We are prepared to allow you to leave our star system, but the Mulbor Kray will remain here."

"Relinquish our vessel or we will attack," replied Hylak.

"Your power systems will not allow for an extended attack," said Frank. "We took as much of your energy cells as we could find and destroyed the collection facility. If you attack us, win or lose, you well be stuck here forever. Again, we will let you leave."

Hylak sent an instruction to one of his Cains, "Understood," returned the Dar'Wannian pilot. He immediately brought his Cain to the front of their formation and aimed very carefully at the Mulbor's cargo bay. A single blast from the Cain tore a hole in the side of the Mulbor and Frank ordered a retaliation of two tach birds, "Put this one down," he ordered over the human's com-link network.

The two tach birds exited the Mulbor and flew straight at the Cains. The men hanging outside the tach birds aimed their tubes at the offending Cain and fired simultaneously.

The Cain was struck by both energy blasts, immediately killing both the pilot and co-pilot.

Hylak was furious and ordered the tach birds be destroyed at once. As soon as the tach birds had fired on the Cain, they turned and moved away from the front line of their formation. The Cains, in pursuit flew past the Mulbor, and four additional tach birds exited the Mulbor falling in behind the Cains. The energy tubes on two tach birds were directed at the Cains. The two men holding the tubes were slightly off target with their first round. The second proved more accurate, knocking the Cains off balance and allowing a third and fatal volley fired by the second pair of tach birds. All the tach birds were now out of the Mulbor and engaging the Cains from both Tarb vessels.

The Karnis Tarb moved toward the Mulbor Kray. Not knowing if they would attack the Mulbor, Darce and Jason aboard the Blue Wolf set out in pursuit. The Karnis fired a blast at the Mulbor, opening another hole in the Mulbor's cargo area, killing three humans and wounding several others. The cargo bay was now open to outer space and as the temperature dropped and air escaped, the remaining humans rushed for sealed compartments where they would be safe.

Linsman turned the Mulbor in a long arc and the main energy cannon was aimed at the Karnis. A single blast from the cannon, directed at the Karnis hit a Cain as it passed in the line of fire and obliterated it. The Karnis responded with another hit to the cargo bay that left another opening.

"They're firing on us," said Hansby, "I thought they wanted the Mulbor back—intact."

"I think they are willing to take it with limited damage, these few hits put relatively small holes in the cargo area outer walls, but not enough to disable the vessel," said Linsman. "I just hope they don't target the bridge."

*   *   *

2246.04.06.14.38 (Off-World)   Aboard the Mulbor Kray

The Blue Wolf sighted two Cains and prepared to open fire on them. Jason, in an EMU, opened the top hatch, aimed his energy tube at one of the Cains and squeezed. The blast struck the side of the Cain and knocked it off course, but it recovered and turned to attack. He fired a second blast, this time striking the front view port of the Cain, killing the pilot and sending the vessel spiraling out of control. "That's seven down and five to go," said Jason.

The Karnis saw the Blue Wolf take out the Cain and turned to attack, "I think Hylak heard you," said Darce. "What's your energy level?"

"Not enough to take on the Karnis," said Jason, "I gotta get outta this damn suit. Be right with you."

"The Karnis is coming this way, and I assume they're low on energy as well," said Darce.

"We have enough power so, let's take 'em for a ride, burn up their fuel," suggested Jason.

Darce looked at Jason, smiled and said, "Hang on, I'm gonna try a little loop."

The Blue Wolf accelerated in a straight line away from the Mulbor and Karnis. The Karnis immediately set their sights on the Blue Wolf and followed in pursuit. At a distance of ninety-seven kilometers, Darce fired the forward lift thrusters, and the Blue Wolf began a sharp incline that continued in a complete circular loop bringing the Wolf behind the Karnis. As the Karnis tried to duplicate the move by the Wolf, their main engine sputtered in the failed attempt and flew off in a tangential path toward the void of deep space.

"Are they outta juice?" posed Jason.

"Looks like it," said Darce, "juice and luck. I don't think we could catch them and do any good. They're lost."

2246.04.06.16.49 (Off-World)   Aboard the Karnis Tarb

Hylak and Bynton went through a complete energy check, "We've drained the energy supply to the engines. All we have now is our life-support system and maybe two or three weapon discharges."

The Karnis Tarb continued toward the Kuiper belt and Hylak took the weapons control station. He found the Blue Wolf on his scanner and directed the remaining energy to the main cannon. "Bynton, how much power is in the weapon?"

"Enough, but at this distance, it would take a direct hit to destroy them," returned Bynton, "can we maneuver closer?"

"I'll need some of the power to turn and improve our chances," said Hylak as he bled some power from the weapons and directed it to the main engine. The Karnis slowly turned and gently accelerated toward the Blue Wolf.

"We're down to minimal power in the weapon system, Commander," said Bynton.

"I'll return all power to the weapons again," said Hylak. "Do you have them in your sights?"

"They're coming into range," said Bynton. "Soon I'll have them locked in."

"What is our distance now," asked Hylak.

"Twenty-two kilometers and closing," said Bynton. "When we are at twelve, that will be close enough to release the blast."

Hylak checked the scanner and said, "Nineteen, seventeen...are we ready to fire?"

"On your command," replied Bynton.

"Thirteen, twelve…" The blast drained the last of the energy and the Karnis Tarb went dark and silent.

2246.04.06.17.07 (Zulu) Aboard the Blue Wolf

The blast struck the Wolf next to the main engine and the Wolf lost all control. It too was adrift in space heading for the Kuiper Belt.

Jason looked at Darce, "Damn Captain, seems like that sucker got the last word."

Darce looked at his friend, "I'm not giving up yet," as he looked around the Wolf interior.

Jason opened a locker and pulled out a nuke, "Ya know Cap, if this little firecracker were to go off about a few hundred meters that way," he said pointing toward the Kuiper Belt, "it might just push us back toward the Earth."

"You think?" quizzed Darce. "I think it's a big maybe," said Jason. "You got any better ideas?"

"Nope," returned Darce. "Let's give it a try."

2246.04.06.18.49 (Zulu) Aboard the Blue Wolf

"We may not be able to recapture all the tach birds with all this damage," said Frank Linsman. He tapped his com-link, "Tach birds, be advised we are damaged and may not be able to accept all birds back on board. Check your fuel levels. If you can make it back to either SW 26 or 27, please advise. We are waiting to hear from all birds."

Two tach birds limped back to the Mulbor and the pilots remained in their cockpits with only life support running. Two other tach birds made it safely to SW-27.

"Any word from the Blue Wolf?" asked Frank Linsman.

"Nothing," replied Hansby, "it doesn't look good for them."

Tetra paced back and forth, constantly looking at the long-range sensors, "If they were still functioning, we'd have a signal, but there's nothing."

Hansby was startled as an explosion was detected approximately fifty-thousand kilometers out. "What was that?" he blurted. "I thought the battle was over."

2246.04.06.19.53 (Zulu) Aboard the Blue Wolf

"How much radiation hit us with that little nuke?" asked Darce.

"I don't know," replied Jason. "Hopefully not enough to kill us, but if we do make it, we may be quarantined for a month or two."

"On the brighter side, we have life support, a few lights and some small power tool capability," said Jason. "So, let's fix this buggy and get it back to Tetra. She'd be very pissed if we lost her favorite toy."

Darce smiled and said, "Okay, what's first?"

"The communication system,' said Jason. "Let's get it up and running and send a signal so someone can come get us."

As they worked on reconnecting various wiring in the main engine compartment, different indicators came to life. One of the first was the Oxygen sensor. The readings began to slowly drop when the Wolf was hit. The same for nitrogen and other gasses.

Jason opened all the passageways trying to add as much oxygen to the mix as possible and they continued to make repairs. Darce opened a locker and found the second energy container and converter they received from the Dar'Wannians, "Jason, lookie here, a bonus."

Darce held a charged trouble light as Jason disconnected the nearly spent energy cylinder and began to insert the new one. "I thought they said we should cut all circuits before we installed a new power cylinder," said Darce, "then bring the systems back online one at a time."

Jason looked at Darce, "True that," and he opened the power panel cutting each circuit. The new power cylinder installed, Jason began slowly closing the important circuits and several systems came back to life. "Darce, try the com-link."

Darce pushed the com-link, "SW-27 or SW-26 come in please. This is the Blue Wolf. Our current location is somewhere above sector 270–280 coming in on a gravitational path toward Earth, engines have no power we have limited control. Please help."

2246.04.06.21.34 (Zulu) Aboard SW-26

"Colonel Hansby, we have a distress message, kinda broken up, but it's the Blue Wolf," said a tech.

"Where are they," demanded Hansby.

"Probably closer to SW-27, sir," returned the tech as he brought up a view of space on the main screen. He placed a red circle on a location about fifty-thousand kilometers above sector 270 and scanned between 270 and 280. "I think they're somewhere in this area."

"Condition?" asked Hansby.

"The message was garbled, but I'm sure they said they have limited control."

"Send a squad of tach birds to search that area and be sure they have tow-lines and EMUs."

Hansby tapped his com-link, "Blue Wolf, this is Hansby, please activate the locator beacon if still working."

2246.04.06.22.56 (Zulu) Aboard the Blue Wolf

Darce looked at Jason, "Locator beacon was my first check—burned out." He paused for a moment before continuing, "Let's send a few tube blasts out, they may see that."

"Anything is worth a try at this point," said Jason as he positioned a tube at the top hatch and started to put the spacesuit on again.

Darce tapped his com-link, "SW, this is Blue Wolf, locator beacon is out, we will send low level energy tube blasts out our top hatch. Should be visible, we hope."

Jason fully suited up tapped his com-link, "Darce, I'm ready to pop the top hatch. Are you secured in the cockpit?"

"Affirmative," returned Darce. "How many blasts do you think we have?"

"At a low level, we probably have fifteen to twenty on each tube," said Jason. "Problem is I have to take off half the damn suit to change armbands between each tube."

"Copy that," said Darce. "How about a minute pause between blasts?"

"Let's make it two minutes," returned Jason. "Ready to get the show started?"

"On my zero," said Darce as he tapped his com-link again. "SW we will begin tube blasts every two minutes beginning in 3, 2, 1, 0."

Jason fired the first blast on the zero count and checked his Chronometer. Two minutes later he fired the second blast.

2246.04.07.02.31 (Zulu) Aboard SW-26

"Colonel, tach bird squad is away. SW-27 is also sending a limited squad," said a tech. "It's all they have operational."

"Copy that," said Hansby, "any sighting of their blasts?"

"Nothing yet Colonel, we'll keep the view on the main screen as we search."

2246.04.07.03.48 (Zulu) Aboard the Blue Wolf

Twenty minutes into the series of blasts, Jason said, "Darce, I think I see a line of lights at our ten o'clock high. Are you getting anything on our scanners?"

“Scanners still very iffy,” said Darce. “Something is blipping in and out, I’ll keep at it,” he paused, “ten o’clock high? That’s the wrong direction!”

2246.04.07.03.51 (Off-World) Aboard the Borstor Tarb

“Is that the Blue Wolf?” demanded Sajten Nostog.

“Most of their systems are down, Commander, but the distress signal we intercepted would seem to indicate so.”

“Prepare weapons,” commanded Nostog. “We will be sure that one is dead, then we find the Mulbor.”

The Borstor moved slowly toward the Blue Wolf as their weapons were brought to bear.

2246.04.07.04.31 (Zulu) Aboard the Blue Wolf

Darce continued to fidget with the scanners and finally said aloud, “That’s not our cavalry, it’s a damn Tarb.”

Jason aimed his tube at the lights and said “Darce, I’m set on low energy with this tube. Any blast from this would bounce off their hull. We still have a nuke—can we fire the damn thing?”

“If you can get back inside and program the missile.”

“Comin’ in, give me a hand with this suit,” said Jason as he pulled the top hatch closed and locked it.

Darce opened the cockpit hatch and pulled himself through, took the helmet from Jason and pulled the top of the suit down past his arms, “I’ll get the nuke out and over to the launch gear.”

Jason looked at the scanner screen at the approaching Tarb and immediately opened the access panel on the nuke. A few entries in its control system and he secured the access panel. They moved the missile into the launch mechanism and Jason tried to aim the missile, but the Blue Wolf’s launch system was not fully functional. “I’ll have to do this manually. Outside!”

“Are you sure?” asked Darce.

"Nope," said Jason, "you have a better idea?" Darce looked at his friend and shook his head.

"Okay," said Jason, "take off the locks inside here while I suit up again. I'll point the damn thing at the Tarb and get outta the way, then you hit the launch button and I'll get back inside." He paused, looked at the pile of energy tubes and picked up one that was fully charged. "Just in case," he said as he strapped on the armband and pulled on the rest of the suit.

Darce went back into the cockpit and brought up the launch system on his control panel. "Jason, I'm ready when you're clear."

Jason maneuvered outside, crawled under the belly of the Wolf, and manually turned the missile to point directly at the Tarb. He crawled back on top of the Wolf and positioned himself halfway in the top hatch, then took the energy tube and said, "Fire when ready Darce."

Darce looked at the faint image of the Borstor Tarb, said, "Goodnight," and pushed the launch button.

Jason watched the missile streak toward the Tarb. He programmed the missile to detonate when within 100 meters of the target. The wait seemed endless, then a bright flash and Jason ducked inside the Blue Wolf as the shockwave hit and rocked the Wolf. He again peered out the top hatch, brought his energy tube up as well and searched for the Tarb.

Darce blurted over the com-link, "We got him, Jason, but he's still viable."

2246.04.07.04.46 (Off-World) Aboard the Borstor Tarb

"Status," demanded Nostog, "do we still have weapons?"

"Making adjustments now," returned the soldier. "Almost ready."

"How many blast capabilities do we have left?"

"At most, three," said the soldier, "but at least two at full power."

"Prepare to fire," said Nostog.

"Another moment, Commander," returned the soldier. "Our targeting system is still not operating properly."

"Can you direct the weapon manually?"

"Yes, Commander."

"Let me know when you're ready," said Nostog.

2246.04.07.05.16 (Zulu)   Aboard the Blue Wolf

"They're probably getting ready to fire," said Jason, "I'll give him another shot with one of their own toys." He carefully aimed the energy tube at the on-coming Tarb, "Kinda like a cockroach, Darce, ya gotta step on him twice."

2246.04.07.05.34 (Off-World)   Aboard the Borstor Tarb

"Weapons system ready, Commander."

As Nostog was about to order the weapon discharge, another blast from the Blue Wolf struck the Tarb, tearing a hole in its passenger bay.

"Seal all compartments," screamed Nostog. "And prepare to fire!"

The blast disrupted the sighting of the main weapon and as the Tarb fired, the blast missed the Blue Wolf by a distance of at least a hundred meters.

"Prepare to fire again," ordered Nostog.

2246.04.07.05.46 (Zulu)   Aboard the Blue Wolf

"They won't miss like that again," said Darce.

Jason was already back inside re-arming himself with another energy tube. "We've got one more of these things at full power if we need it, and if I can re-arm quick enough." He hurried through the re-arming and started for the top hatch.

Darce closed the cockpit hatch and checked his monitors again. The two squadrons of tach birds were on their way, but still at a distance and wouldn't be there in time to be involved in the battle.

Jason stood halfway out of the top hatch and aimed his weapon. The Tarb was now closer but still too far to sight any specific part of the vessel. He very calmly aimed the tube and squeezed. The blast crossed the empty space in an instant and struck the Tarb near one of its control engines, pushing it slightly off course.

2246.04.07.05.53 (Off-world) Aboard the Borstor Tarb

"Commander we're hit again," said a soldier as Nostog pushed the weapons discharge button. The blast caught part of the Blue Wolf's side doing damage, but not enough to destroy the Wolf.

"How much energy do we have left for our weapon?" demanded Nostog.

"We're down to less than half power, Commander."

"Prepare to fire again."

"Commander, that will drain all our power and we won't be able to maneuver or maintain life systems."

"Again, prepare to fire," said Nostog. "This battle was lost before we attacked them, Soldier. We are not going to win, but we will take that damn Blue Wolf with us in defeat."

"Yes, Commander," returned the soldier, "we cannot aim the tube, it's frozen at an angle over thirty degrees to our starboard side."

"In order to direct the energy burst at them, we must maneuver this vessel into a different position," said the soldier. "We must come to a new heading of twenty-five degrees from our heading and a two-degree rise so the tube is pointing directly at the Blue Wolf. I will let you know when we are ready to fire."

Nostog looked at the view screen and said, "We'll wait 'til we're closer and we can't miss. Then we will have our small victory."

2246.04.07.06.17 (Zulu) Aboard the Blue Wolf

"Last energy tube, Darce. They'll be too close to miss again so, I'll have to fire first."

Darce nodded, "Aim well, my friend." He closed the cockpit hatch and watched the view screen. The Borster Tarb was now about a thousand meters away.

"Aim well," repeated Darce, quietly to himself.

Jason shouldered the tube and sighted it on the center of the Tarb where the cockpit should be. He hesitated, wondering how long he could wait, how long he should wait. Then, as the Tarb seemed to be stabilizing, "Like they're ready to fire," muttered Jason as he squeezed the tube, ducked inside, and pulled the hatch closed.

Darce saw the blast from the tube streak across the void like a perfectly straight bolt of lightning and strike the Borstor Tarb near the center of the bridge, causing the vessel to shudder, veer slightly off course, and drift toward the Blue Wolf.

2246.04.07.06.54 (Off-world) Aboard the Borstor Tarb

As the blast ripped through the bridge, the atmosphere was torn away, and the crew was left gasping for air. The main power systems were down, and most control panels no longer functioned. Nostog furiously entered commands to no avail and looked toward a hatch leading to another compartment where air might be found. He realized he'd never make it and lost consciousness struggling to release his securing straps.

The Borstor continued drifting past the Blue Wolf missing a collision by less than twenty meters. The remaining crew aboard the Tarb were sectioned off in several compartments, where the air supply might last a few hours. They were not able to return to the bridge or any other point of control. Try as they might, no controls or systems responded properly. The last sparks of power in the weapons system slowly migrated through the firing sequence and the main energy tube, no longer directed at the Blue Wolf, released its final burst. The blast flew across empty space toward the Kuiper Belt where it would likely strike and destroy an asteroid.

Battle can be hell…the Blue Wolf had won this encounter and now the living souls aboard the Borster Tarb peering out through the vessel's side viewports would pay the ultimate price of loss. Their Tarb was without power, drifting aimlessly into space at the mercy of gravity and chance.

2246.04.07.07.05 (Zulu) Aboard the Blue Wolf

Darce helped Jason out of the EMU, and they sat together watching the two squads of tach birds surround them, attach tow lines and start for SW-27.

NINETEEN

2246.04.07.53.47 (Zulu) Aboard the SW-26

Colonel Hansby called Tetra into the main control room, "In case you're interested Major, it appears the Blue Wolf has been recovered with two young men aboard."

Tetra looked relieved, "Thank you, Colonel."

"I'll be taking a shuttle over to SW-27 in an hour," said Hansby. "Would you care to join me?"

"Thank you. I'd like that."

2246.04.08.24.08 (Zulu) Aboard the SW-27

"Major Harmon, Colonel Hansby, welcome aboard," said General Kearsay. "I assume you'd like to see our two Marines."

Hansby led Kearsay into an office and said, "Let's give them a few minutes."

"Understood," said Kearsay, "I think I have all I need from them."

* * *

Tetra entered the medical wing of the station carrying a small duffle. She saw Dr. Morrison. "Jan, how are your patients doing?" she asked.

"We lost a few people out there, Major. But thanks to you and those two over there," she said, pointing across the room, "we're home and didn't lose more."

"Thanks, Jan," and she hurried across the floor. "Hi, guys."

Darce and Jason both sat up straight on their beds, "Tetra."

She looked at Jason and said, "Good to see you made it back." Then she walked over to Darce, "Captain Gannon, I'd like to discuss the damage you did to my Blue Wolf."

Jason smiled as he stood and looked at Jan Morrison, "Am I good to go, Doc?"

"You are. Check in with me or someone here or on the surface in a week. We'll run some fresh labs and be sure nothing else is wrong."

Tetra stepped closer to Darce as he stood. She touched his hand and said, "I really am glad you came back."

Jason finished buttoning his shirt and said, "Shore leave, Cap, at least three weeks, and I'm gonna find me a storm."

Darce replied, "Yeah, I'll see you in three weeks." He looked at Tetra, "Wanna go up to the observation deck and look at the stars?"

"Sure, but first, let's stop in my quarters. I have to drop this off," she said, holding up her duffle.

As he walked out of the medical wing, Jason was muttering a tune about thunder and lightning.

Darce looked at Tetra, "He's into storms."

She looked at Darce, squeezed his hand, and said, "Yeah, me too."

* * *

END

www.ingramcontent.com/pod-product-compliance
Ingram Content Group UK Ltd.
Pitfield, Milton Keynes, MK11 3LW, UK
UKHW012249290726
14090UKWH00013B/548